ALEA JACTA EST !

GOSCINNY AND UDERZO
PRESENT
AN ASTERIX GAME BOOK

THE MEETING OF
THE CHIEFTAINS

TRANSLATED BY ANTHEA BELL

HODDER AND STOUGHTON
LONDON SYDNEY AUCKLAND TORONTO

GEOGRAPHICAL GLOSSARY

Aquae Calidae	Vichy
the Arvernian countryside	the Auvergne
Burdigala	Bordeaux
Condatum	Rennes
Lugdunum	Lyons
Lusitania	Portugal
Lutetia	Paris
Mediolanum	Milan

British Library Cataloguing in Publication Data

Uderzo
The meeting of the chieftains: Goscinny and Uderzo
present an Asterix game book
1. French humorous strip cartoons. Collections from
individual artists. English texts
I. Title   II. Goscinny, *1926-1977*   III. Series
IV. Le Rendez-vous du chef. English
741.5'944

ISBN 0-340-50384-X

Original edition © Editions Albert René, Goscinny-Uderzo, 1988
English translation © Editions Albert René, Goscinny-Uderzo, 1989
Exclusive licensee: Hodder and Stoughton Ltd
Translator: Anthea Bell

First published in Great Britain 1989

Published by Hodder and Stoughton Children's Books,
a division of Hodder and Stoughton Ltd,
Mill Road, Dunton Green, Sevenoaks, Kent TN13 2YA

Typeset by SX Composing, Rayleigh, Essex

Printed in Belgium by Proost International Book Production

GAULISH VILLAGE

COMPENDIUM

LAUDANUM

AQUARIUM

TOTORUM

ARMORICA

BELGICA

LUTETIA

SPQR

GAUL
(ROMAN CONQUEST)
50 B.C.

CELTICA

PROVINCIA

AQUITANIA

The year is 50 BC. Gaul is entirely occupied by the Romans. Well, not entirely . . . One small village of indomitable Gauls still holds out against the invaders. And life is not easy for the Roman legionaries who garrison the fortified camps of Totorum, Aquarium, Laudanum and Compendium . . .

ALEA JACTA EST !

HERE IS A NEW KIND OF ASTERIX BOOK . . .

YOU ARE JUSTFORKIX, THE HERO OF THIS STORY. YES, YOU
YOURSELF ARE JUSTFORKIX, A YOUNG MAN FROM LUTETIA. WE
KNOW SOMETHING ABOUT YOU ALREADY, FROM 'ASTERIX AND
THE NORMANS'. IN THAT BOOK, YOUR FATHER SENT YOU TO THE
LITTLE GAULISH VILLAGE TO TOUGHEN YOU UP A BIT. MAYBE YOU
DON'T HAVE QUITE THE STRENGTH OF OBELIX, OR THE WISDOM
OF GETAFIX, OR EVEN THE EXPERIENCE OF ASTERIX, BUT
NOBODY'S PERFECT . . .

AND YOU ARE NOW ABOUT TO FACE DREADFUL DANGERS. FROM
PARAGRAPH TO PARAGRAPH, FROM PERIL TO PERIL, YOU WILL
HAVE TO MAKE DIFFICULT DECISIONS, TAKE RISKY ACTION,
THROW THE DICE AND SEE WHAT LUCK CHANCE BRINGS YOU, GET
YOURSELF OUT OF COMPLICATED SITUATIONS, SOLVE KNOTTY
PROBLEMS. YOU WON'T ALWAYS BE SUCCESSFUL . . . AND IF YOU
AREN'T, YOU WILL HAVE TO BEGIN THE ADVENTURE AGAIN.

BUT NEVER DESPAIR! REMEMBER THAT YOU ARE AN
INDOMITABLE GAUL . . .

YOU WERE BORN IN LUTETIA NOT SO VERY LONG AGO . . . YOUR PARENTS WERE SURE YOU WERE DESTINED FOR GREAT THINGS . . .

SON, YOU WILL BE A SENATOR, AN EXPLORER, A GENERAL, A BARD . . .

. . . STRONG, SKILFUL, HANDSOME . . .

TODAY, ALL YOUR PARENTS' HOPES HAVE COME TRUE. ALL OF THEM?

NO. TO BE HONEST, YOUR COURAGE AND STRENGTH OF CHARACTER HAVE HARDLY BEEN PUT TO THE TEST . . .

SCREEEEECH!

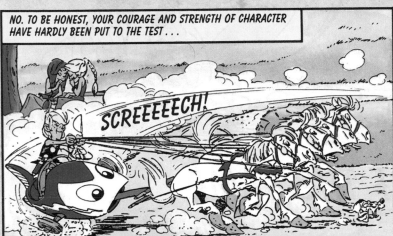

BUT NEVER MIND THAT! YOUR FATHER SENT YOU TO SEE UNCLE VITALSTATISTIX, WHO LIVES IN A LITTLE VILLAGE WE ALL KNOW WELL . . .

A VILLAGE WHERE TRUE GAULS INTRODUCED YOU TO A MAN'S LIFE . . .

. . . TAUGHT YOU HOW TO FIGHT . . .

LET 'EM COME! LET 'EM ALL COME!

. . . IN EVERY KIND OF WAY . . .

BOO!

. . . AND HELPED YOU TO TAKE DIFFICULT DECISIONS.

CHATTER - -CHAT -TER!

YOU HAVE FOUND THAT CERTAIN CIRCUMSTANCES LEND YOU WINGS . . .

. . . AND SOMETIMES EVEN COURAGE!

BOING! BOING! BOING!

AND NOW, AT LAST, YOU ARE READY FOR YOUR GREAT ADVENTURE. ALEA JACTA EST!

RULES OF THE GAME

You are going to have a thrilling and dangerous adventure in this book; you can be sure of that! But you may not be quite so sure how to play it yet.

So read the following rules carefully. They apply to all the ASTERIX game books in this series. They are clear and simple – don't hesitate to turn to them during the game if necessary.

CHANCE BOARD

All you need to play the game is this book, a pencil, and an eraser so that you can rub pencil marks out and play the game again. If you happen to have a dice, that's fine. But don't worry if you haven't. You can use the Chance Board which you will find at the end of the book.

ADVENTURE SLAB

You take the Adventure Slab with you on your adventures. It will come in useful when you want to note something down as a reminder, leaving you free to put your mind to other problems. You can detach it from the rest of the book, and then you get two for the price of one.

PERSONAL QUALITIES

Take a look at your Adventure Slab. You start out with three personal qualities.
● *Skill.*
● *Fighting Fitness.*
● *Charm.*

Each quality carries a number of points. It's up to you to decide on your own personality knowing that:
– you already have 10 points for each quality,
– you have an extra 15 points to divide between your qualities at the beginning of the adventure.

Record your choice on the Adventure Slab. Adding up the number of points your three qualities carry, you should get 45. If you don't get 45, either you've made a mistake or you've been cheating already!

SECONDARY APTITUDES

Needless to say, you weren't born yesterday, and you've already knocked about Gaul a bit. So you've learnt some useful little tricks to use from day to day. At the beginning of the adventure, and sometimes in the middle of it, you will be told to choose between various aptitudes. Select whichever seems to you most useful, and don't forget to write it down on your Adventure Slab.

OBJECTS

A good legionary never goes anywhere without equipment. You can choose various objects which may turn out useful during your adventure, though on the other hand they may be more of a nuisance than anything else. And you can take only 5 objects. If you come across some other object during your travels and you want to take it with you, but you already have 5, you must get rid of one of them. You will find out what objects you can take in one of the early chapters.

NB: the gourd of magic potion and the purse of sestertii do not count as objects. They are extra items of equipment.

FIGHTS

Knowing you, you're bound to find yourself in situations where a punch-up or a spot of sword-play is called for.

To find out the result of your fights, follow these rules:

1. Enter your Fighting Fitness points in one of the Fights spaces on your Adventure Slab, plus any points that certain objects earn you – for instance, a sword or a shield.

2. Now write down your enemy's points. (You will find these given in the text.)

3. Throw the dice, or use the Chance Board, and subtract the number you get from your enemy's points score.

4. Throw the dice again, and subtract the number you get from your own score.

5. Carry on in the same way until your score or your enemy's score reaches 0. The loser is whichever of you reaches 0 first.

6. Unless there is any instruction telling you otherwise, you start again with the same original number of points next time you fight.

Example: a centurion takes you by surprise and challenges you to a duel. Suppose your score for Fighting Fitness is 15 and the centurion's score is 12. If you also have a sword (+5) and a shield (+3), your actual score for Fighting Fitness is thus 15+5+3 = 23.

Well done! You have won this particular fight . . . but it might not always be so easy.

NB: your Skill or Charm may also be used in a fight, depending on circumstances. When the time to use them comes, of course, you will be told.

FIGHTS AGAINST MORE THAN ONE ENEMY

In fights of this kind, you will be told either your enemies' total Fighting Fitness, and you have only one fight, or their individual Fighting Fitness, and you have more than one fight on your hands. But a word of warning . . . when fighting two enemies separately, and only then, you do not get your original Fighting Fitness score back to fight the second; you start with whatever points you have left from the first of the two fights.

TESTS

In certain other circumstances you may not have to fight an enemy, but you still have to pass a test of Skill, Fighting Fitness or Charm, using those qualities to get yourself out of a tricky situation. When that happens, follow these rules:

1. Always write down your points score for whichever quality is concerned, plus any extra points certain objects give you.

2. The degree of difficulty will always be given for each test, for instance: *difficulty 4*.

3. Now throw the dice as many times as the degree of difficulty indicates, for instance: *difficulty 4* = 4 throws of the dice, *difficulty 5* = 5 throws.

4. Each time you throw the dice, subtract the number you get from your own points score.

5. If you are left with a number above 0, you have succeeded. If you get 0 or a minus number, you have failed.

6. Unless you are told otherwise, you start again with your original points score when the next test comes up.

Example: you have to pass a test of skill with a difficulty factor of 4. You start with 14 points for Skill. You throw the dice 4 times and subtract the number from 14; for instance, $14-3-5-1-3 = 2$. As the result is above 0, you have succeeded.

MAGIC POTION

If you drink some of Getafix's magic potion, you automatically win a fight or succeed in a test of your Fighting Fitness without needing to follow the usual rules. When the fight or the test is over, you lose your superhuman strength. You will then have to face the next fight or test in the usual way, unless you drink another dose of magic

potion. Your gourd holds five doses at the beginning of your adventure.

Remember that:
– The magic potion will not work in fights or tests which call for you to use your personal qualities of Skill or Charm.

– You can drink magic potion only at the beginning of a fight or a test, never in the middle of it.

Keep a record of the number of doses of potion left in your gourd on your Adventure Slab.

PURSE

You are sure to need money on your travels. You must keep careful note of the number of sestertii you spend on your Adventure Slab.

THE END OF THE ADVENTURE

Sometimes, when you have lost a fight or made an error of judgment, you will read the fateful words: 'YOUR ADVENTURE IS OVER'.

Then you must start again at Chapter I.

CHAPTER I

ON HOLIDAY FROM LUTETIA

Worn out with the pace of life in Lutetia, the traffic jams, the amphoranecks*, you have decided to take your father Doublehelix's advice and go for a holiday in a little village in Armorica you already know well. On previous visits to the village, you could have learned business skills from Unhygienix, livestock-rearing from Bucolix, hunting from Obelix. Your experience of the night life of Lutetia may have given you a good head for drink. *Choose one of these four Secondary Aptitudes (business skills, livestock-rearing, hunting, a good head for drink) and write it on your Adventure Slab.*

The journey from Lutetia was uneventful. You looked splendid in your magnificent red sports chariot made in Mediolanum. Despite the price of fodder, which has risen steeply recently, you still have 35 sestertii in the purse Doublehelix gave you when you left. *(Write this sum of money down on your Adventure Slab.)*
The man on guard outside the village gates dives for the ditch just in time; you are urging your horses on full speed ahead, to impress the villagers . . . but as you gallop through the gates, a wheel comes off your chariot and . . . CRAAAASH! By Toutatis! You're not injured yourself, but the chariot is damaged. Hearing the noise, the villagers all run out, while you make your way towards Uncle Vitalstatistix's house, feeling rather crestfallen.
● Go to **1**.
*Ancient Gaulish bottle-necks.

Impedimenta welcomes you with open arms. You were always her favourite nephew. 'Justforkix, dear, how are you? You must be worn out after such a long journey! What a shame your uncle isn't here at the moment! Have you had anything to eat? There's a boar roasting this very minute. Or maybe you'd like a nice bath first? I'll just go and draw water from the village well!' There is no chance of making yourself scarce for the time being. You hug your aunt, and decide:
● You aren't really hungry; you'd rather have a bath. Go to **20**.
● You can't resist Impedimenta's tempting suggestion. Go to **14**.

In the village square, the villagers are all going about their business just as usual. You can go (if you haven't been already):
- To see your friends Asterix and Obelix. Go to **26**.
- To see Getafix the druid. Go to **17**.
- To see Geriatrix. Go to **21**.
- Back to Impedimenta's. Go to **24**.
- Or if you know where Vitalstatistix has gone, you can go and look for him at **30**.

3

Nothing like a nice punch-up to get the stiffness out of your joints! PAF! POF! Everyone is happily thumping everyone else. If only your friends from Lutetia's Latin Quarter could see you now! Missiles of every kind are zooming through the air. *Take a test of Fighting Fitness (difficulty 4).*
- If you succeed, go to **27**.
- If you fail, go to **15**.

4

Well fancy that – a Roman legionary! Crouching in the ditch which surrounds the village, the Roman is watching everything going on in the square through a gap in the fence. A spy! And in camouflage gear, too (at least, he has a few twigs stuck in his helmet). On seeing you he is about to turn and run for it. It's up to you to decide whether to fight him or let him go.
- You let him go and return to the village. Go to **2**.
- You decide to fight. If you win, go to **16**. If you lose, go to **15**. *(The Roman has 20 points for Fighting Fitness. At any moment you can stop hitting your enemy and call the villagers to your aid. In that case you miss a throw of the dice, your enemy has another throw, you have a throw, and then your enemy has a last throw. If neither of you has won the fight, go to **9**.)*

5

'You young scamp, Justforkix, you're acting like a savage! Fighting in the street, at your age! I thought young people in Lutetia were better-behaved than the barbarians we get here, but I can see I was wrong. I shall tell Doublehelix!' Impedimenta threatens.
- You get back into the tub. Go to **10**.

6

'Gergovia, ah, those were the days! I fought at Gergovia myself, you know. What a thrashing we gave the Romans! That was a battle, that was, the battle of Gergovia! And we didn't have any magic potion at Gergovia, no, indeed! I can still remember how we were besieged with Vercingetorix in our fortified town by the Romans. Caesar's armies were camping to the north of the town, and we couldn't get out on the south side, because the town itself was built on cliffs. The Romans never managed to get in. What's more, young Justforkix, some of us Gauls dug tunnels which came out on the other side of the ramparts, so that we could attack Caesar's troops by night without opening the town gates. Yes, Gergovia was quite something! Not like today's campaigning, with magic potion and all mod cons! I feel really sorry for the young folk of today! Here, see that sword above the hearth? That's the sword I fought with at Gergovia. I'll lend it to you if you like. Mind you take care of it – that sword was at Gergovia, and it's seen more Romans than you have! I wouldn't mind going back to Gergovia some day, you know. I had a friend there, Localpolitix his name was, he stayed on after the siege and started a little business. I should have done the same. See you again soon, young Justforkix. You must come and have a boar with us, and I'll tell you all about the Gallic War. Ah, Gergovia, what a battle that was.'
- Relieved to find you don't have to listen to the full tale of the Gallic War just yet, you leave Geriatrix's house and go back to **2**. *(You can add the sword to your equipment.)*

'One doesn't leave the table before the end of a meal, Justforkix! You haven't finished your second boar. Don't they teach you any manners in Lutetia these days? I won't have you fighting with those guttersnipes!'
• You can't be rude to Impedimenta after such a good meal. Go to **22**.

The messenger, turning to go back, takes the road which leads to the village of Chief Whosemoralsarelastix. It is perched on a cliff several milia passuum* away. Thrilled by your own boldness, you follow him at a distance. You are just going through the village gates when you hear a faint cracking sound to your left, near the fence.
• You go on following the messenger, taking more precautions. *Take a test of Skill (difficulty 4)*. If you succeed, go to **19**. If you fail, go to **11**.
• You decide to tackle the messenger and talk to him, hoping to find out more about Chief Whosemoralsarelastix and the details of this strange meeting. Go to **23**.
• You stop following and go to **4** to find out where the strange noise is coming from.
*The Romans measured distance in feet. One mille passuum was a thousand feet, or one Roman mile.

AAAAARRGH! A dozen furious Gauls, excited by the prospect of a punch-up, rush to your aid. The terrified legionary falls to his knees, crying, 'Mercy! I surrender!'
• Go to **28**.

What a shame! A nice fight is always fun! SPLOSH! A fish which has lost its way falls into your bath-water. What a way to behave! Well, since the least a well-brought-up young man can do is return lost property to its owner, you get out of the tub and throw the fishy missile out of the window again. Yuk! What a horrible smell! Why are the fish always so much fresher in Lutetia, even though this village is by the seaside?

• Your bath has gone on long enough. It's time to go and take a look at what seems to be a pitched battle. Go to **27**.

You follow the Gaul at a distance. The important thing is not to let him notice you. But of course, after going some way you step on a dry twig. CRACK! The messenger turns round. 'Since when have Gauls spied on each other?' he asks. 'I shall tell Chief Whosemoralsarelastix about this!'
• Annoyed, and unable to think of an answer, you go back to the village. Go to **2**.

Getafix asks you to go home with him. He wants a little talk with you.
• Go to **17**.

'Alesia? What d'you mean, Alesia? I don't know anything about Alesia! Nobody knows anything about Alesia! Nobody even knows where Alesia is! Get out of here, you scamp, you guttersnipe, you decadent Gallo-Roman!' You take to your heels and leave the hut. Geriatrix stands outside the door, waving his stick and hurling imprecations at you (and no, they're not something you can pick up and throw back either).
• You make your escape to **2**.

14

How lucky you are to have an aunt who's such a good cook! The roast wild boar is really delicious! What a change from the stuff you usually eat in the Acutae Tabernae* of Lutetia! The taste of boar reminds you of hunting expeditions in the forest with your friends Asterix and Obelix. But an animated discussion interrupts your thoughts. You hear the tuneful voices of the fishmonger Unhygienix and the blacksmith Fulliautomatix.
• It sounds as if there's going to be a good Gaulish punch-up! You can't miss this! Rising, you make for the door. Go to **7**.
• You've only had a boar and a half, and you're still hungry. Too bad about the punch-up; you decide to finish your meal. Go to **22**.

*Gallo-Roman fast food restaurants.

15

Hello, what's all this? No, you're not in your bedroom at home in Lutetia, but in the druid Getafix's house. Your leg hurts. It is covered with poultices of plantain leaves. Getafix is bending over you, a smile lurking somewhere in his white beard. 'Don't worry, Justforkix, it's nothing much. Your leg will soon heal, but you must stay where you are for a week. Here, have some of this potion. It will make you feel better. If you hadn't overestimated your strength, there was a little mission I'd thought of entrusting to you.'
YOUR ADVENTURE IS OVER, before it even began!

16

After you have exchanged a few blows, the legionary collapses, unconscious.
• You wait for him to come round to interrogate him. Go to **28**.
• You go straight back to the village. Go to **2**.

17

'Well, young Justforkix, I'm afraid your uncle's not at home, and nor are your friends Asterix and Obelix,' says Getafix. 'Vitalstatistix hasn't been too well recently. It's his liver, you know. I advised him to take the waters at the hot springs of Aquae Calidae, where my colleague and friend the druid Diagnostix runs a health farm. The chief set off for Aquae Calidae with Asterix and Obelix as escort. However, he isn't back yet, even though the cure he was going to take must have finished several days ago. I'm worried. Vitalstatistix has his traditional meeting with Chief Whosemoralsarelastix, another village chief, in a fortnight's time. Chief Whosemoralsarelastix gets on rather suspiciously well with the Romans. What's more, he's very touchy, and I'm afraid if Vitalstatistix doesn't turn up for their meeting, he'll take it as an insult and an excuse to go over to the Romans. The present peace in Armorica is precarious anyway, and it would be in great danger then. Someone must go to Aquae Calidae to find your uncle. I only hope he's all right . . .'
• Without a moment's hesitation, you volunteer to go to Aquae Calidae and look for Uncle Vitalstatistix. Travel is good for the young. Go to **25**.
• Travel is good for the young, but so are holidays. You say you'd really rather stay in the Gaulish village for the time being. Go to **29**.

18

The fish are flying freely. Here's a traditional Gaulish punch-up! You can hardly imagine such a scene in the big squares of Lutetia. Everyone is thumping each other in a spirit of happiness and good humour.

- Tired after your journey, you go to **27** to watch this quaint and charming Ancient Gaulish tradition, but you do not take part.
- You don't get enough exercise back home in Lutetia. You rush into the thick of the fight. Go to **3**.

19

Hiding behind the trees, you see the Gaul go into Chief Whosemoralsarelastix's house. There are warriors all over the place. It wouldn't be easy to go on with your detective work in the circumstances. And obviously what the messenger said was true.
- Go back to the village, at **2**, and try again.

20

You go to the well with Impedimenta to draw water for your bath. On the way you notice that the hut where your friends Asterix and Obelix live looks unoccupied. Back at your uncle's house, you put the bath-tub in a corner, fill it with water, and get in. The water feels lovely. Snatches of conversation outside the house drift in . . . something about fish which isn't as fresh as it might be . . . Sounds as if there's a punch-up brewing!
- As you really are rather dirty, you finish your bath. Go to **10**.
- It would be a real shame to miss a good brawl! You quietly get out of the bath and get dressed, hoping Impedimenta won't see you leave. *Take a test of Skill (difficulty 3)*. If you succeed, go to **18**. If you fail, go to **5**.

21

'Young man,' says Geriatrix, 'before I teach you a thing or two about our ancestors, let's take a look at modern history. I'm sure that like every good Gaul you know the name of the greatest battle in the Gallic War?'
Easy! You reply:
- 'Alesia.' Go to **13**.
- 'Gergovia.' Go to **6**.

22

After a little polite conversation with Impedimenta, who wants news of her family, your father's business, and the latest Lutetian fashions, you leave the house. In passing, your aunt slips some coins into your hand. Your pleasure is short-lived: only 5 sestertii, hardly worth a thing! Your country cousins seem to think you're still a little boy! Or else they just don't know what prices are like in Lutetia.
- You go to join in the fight at **27**.

23

'Who is this Chief Whosemoralsarelastix?' you ask. 'I've only recently arrived in these parts, and I haven't heard much about him.' 'He's chief of the village on the clifftop,' he replies. 'It's thanks to him we live at peace with the Romans, and with other Gauls too. He's a peace-loving man, but rather touchy. I hope Vitalstatistix isn't going to forget the meeting, because a lot of Gauls, including some of our own villagers, might well regret it . . .' There's no chance of finding out more. However, you know that Chief Whosemoralsarelastix is on good terms with the Romans, and even according to his own messenger he doesn't sound very nice.
- Rather disappointed with your investigation, you leave your companion and go back to the village, at **2**.

24

Impedimenta has left the hut. She must have gone shopping, or out for a goat's milk with some of the other village ladies.
- Go back to **2** and try an alternative decision.

25

'Spoken like a brave Gaul, young man!' says the druid. 'But you mustn't go without some magic potion. Here's a gourd full of the right stuff. Use it as you think best. And take this money too . . . you'll be needing funds. Here's a bag of food as well, and some torches. The most sensible way will be for you to go on foot to Condatum, where you can buy a horse or a chariot.' *Add a gourd of magic potion (5 doses) to your equipment, as well as 30 sestertii, 5 torches (they count as one object), and a bag of food which must last you the journey. Each time you spend any sestertii, drink a dose of magic potion or change any object in your equipment, make a note of it on your Adventure Slab.*
- You now leave Getafix's hut and go back to the village square at **2**.

26

The house where Asterix and Obelix live is closed up. Your holiday is going to be rather dull without them.
- Are you sure? Go back to **2** and try again.

27

Too late! All the Gauls get to their feet, dust themselves down, adjust their clothing and look nonchalant. A stranger has arrived in the village square. Unhygienix collects his fish, ready for next time. The stranger, a Gaul, walks over to the chief's house and announces, 'A message for Chief Vitalstatistix!' Getafix steps forward. 'Our chief's away for a few days,' he says, 'but we can pass the message on.' 'I just came to remind Vitalstatistix that the traditional meeting between the chiefs of our two villages is to take place within our walls in two weeks' time,' says the messenger. 'My chief would be very upset if your chief failed to turn up. He would assume that the friendship between us was at an end, and an alliance with the Romans was inevitable, if not necessary.' Getafix tries to explain, hoping at least to get a respite, but the messenger just turns his back and prepares to leave. This is too much for the wise old druid.

'Personally,' he says, 'I think you're spouting a lot of hot air. We've never trusted Chief Whosemoralsarelastix, not since that business of the cauldron*. I'd like to know what he really has in mind!'
- Eager to use your own initiative, you follow the messenger from Chief Whosemoralsarelastix. This is your chance to find out more. Go to **8**.
- You go to **12** to ask Getafix to explain what's going on. However, the messenger's unexpected visit seems to have put the druid in a bad temper.

*See ASTERIX AND THE CAULDRON.

28

The Roman has a nasty nosebleed. Threatened with another punch on the nose, he admits that he has come from the fortified camp of Totorum. Centurion Voluptuous Arteriosclerosus, commanding the garrison, has heard that Chief Vitalstatistix is not in the village, and sent the legionary on a mission to try to find out where the great chief of the indomitable Gauls has gone. The Romans are out to get your uncle Vitalstatistix.
- You go back to the village at **2**, very thoughtful, while the legionary limps back to Totorum as fast as he can.

29

What bad luck! This could have been the start of a fascinating, exciting story. YOUR ADVENTURE IS OVER, but all the same, you're sure to have a good holiday among your Gaulish friends.

CHAPTER II

AN EVENTFUL START

30

So here you are leaving the Gaulish village early in the afternoon, a bundle over your shoulder. You should be able to get hold of a horse or another chariot easily enough in Condatum. What a pity you've had to leave your own behind because of the smashing effect of your arrival in the village! Just before sunset you come to a small, shady clearing. It looks like a good place to camp.

● You decide to eat some of the provisions Getafix gave you for supper. Go to **65**.

● You go hunting boar in the woods; a nice boar will taste better. *Take a test of Skill (difficulty 4)*. If you succeed, *or* if you have entered hunting as the Secondary Aptitude on your Adventure Slab, go to **95**. If you fail, go to **39**.

31

Getting a foothold on the rough bark of the trunk, you climb up into the branches of a great oak, make yourself a bed of leaves, and soon drop off to sleep. The climb was quite tricky. Have you been rash to set off on this adventure, all by yourself, with only a few sestertii in your purse? You fall asleep and dream of the dangers of the journey: wolves, brigands, even Romans if they find out what your mission is! 'Gaul, I arrest you in the name of Caesar!' You wake up with a start. Phew! It was only a nightmare! *All the same, take a test of Skill (difficulty 4)*.

● If you fail, your rude awakening has unfortunate consequences; you fall out of the tree. Go to **59**.

● If you succeed, you find you soon fall asleep again. Go to **100**.

32

A fat legionary, looking decidedly groggy and walking unsteadily, makes his way towards you brandishing an amphora. He is very drunk, and looks like rousing half the garrison. 'Long live Culius Jaesar! Have a little drink, Gaul! Good for morale!' he says, offering you his amphora.

● Is this wise? Well, a little drink never hurt anyone, and you'd better go along with what this Roman wants or he might raise the alarm. You take the amphora and drink. Go to **92**.

● Better get out of here before the situation gets sticky. You refuse the Roman's generous offer and make for the way out. Go to **98**.

33

Your bonds are rather tight . . . Centurion Arterio-sclerosus, commanding the garrison of Totorum, enters the tent, followed by a legionary and a sinister character carrying pincers, nails, tongs . . . and several slabs, on which you see engraved the words: 'Teach Yourself Tor-turing in Ten Easy Lessons'.

WELL, WELL, A GUEST!!

'Well, Gaul?' bellows the centurion. 'Are you going to tell us where your chief is, or would you rather I called on the services of this man, who has his methods of making you talk? It's no use looking for your gourd. I've got it now, and I plan to investigate its contents. Would they by any chance be that famous magic potion which makes you Gauls invincible?' With some difficulty, you swallow and reply:

● 'Chief Vitalstatistix is in Aquae Calidae. He went there for the good of his health.' Rather a provocative choice, possibly . . . go to **84** and find out what comes of it.

● 'Vitalstatistix is visiting his family in Lutetia.' There are times when a white lie does no harm. Go to **60** to see if the Romans believe you.

● 'My lips are sealed, Roman!' You certainly don't lack courage! Go to **71** and find out what happens to you.

34

Phew! It was a close thing, but you snatched the gourd just before the centurion. Furious, he gets to his feet, draws his sword and attacks. *The centurion's Fighting Fitness score is 30.*

● If you win you leave the tent, but the alarm is raised.
● If you lose the fight, go to **62**.

35

Two legionaries are playing CDXXI*, but they are on the alert. They attack you. *Their Fighting Fitness scores are 18 each, making 36 altogether.*

● If you win the fight, you leave the tent.
● If you lose, go to **62**.

*421.

36

Trembling at the knees, you hide behind a tree. The patrol marches along the road only a little way away from you. Nobody seems to have spotted you. But sud-denly the tall young legionary bringing up the rear turns round. 'Decurion, there's someone behind that oak!' At a sign from the patrol leader, the legionaries turn and surround you, ready to attack!

● You take a dose of magic potion. Go to **40**.
● If you fight them without any potion, go to **94**.

37

You go up to the table. You're in luck . . . or maybe it's just that you have a good memory. Yes, the gourd of magic potion is still there, within the centurion's reach. You only hope he doesn't choose this moment to wake up! Stealthily, you retrieve the gourd and fasten it to your belt. Success! Arteriosclerosus is still snoring.

● You leave the tent.

38

This tent looks like any other, and contains several camp beds. However, as you are leaving you notice some-thing under one of the beds. It's probably just an old caliga.

● You bend down to look under the bed. Go to **101**.
● Why waste time? You're not likely to find anything interesting here. You leave the tent.

39

After chasing vainly about the place you finally hunt out a small wild boar piglet, which takes off through the trees. You are setting off in pursuit when an unexpected shadow looms up, stopping you in your tracks.
● You turn your head, but too late. PAF! You find yourself at **55**.

40

WHAM! BOING! With one blow of your right fist and another of your left you dispose of the Roman patrol. Caesar's legions are not what they used to be. That potion really is magic! You should try it on the Lutetian Roberti* one of these days . . . you make a mental note to tell your friends.
● Feeling cheerful, you continue on your way to **108** as if nothing had happened.
*Gallo-Roman bobbies.

41

'Oi bain't going that far,' he says. 'Oi be off to work in my field beside this here road. Well, best of luck, young feller-me-lad!'
● You part at a crossroads, and you yourself go on along the road to Condatum. Go to **108**.

42

Phew! What luck . . . you caught it just before it fell to the ground. Glancing behind you, you see that Arteriosclerosus has not stirred. You can take the statuette with you, but don't forget it's very heavy. *If you add it to your Adventure Slab, it must count as 2 Objects.*
● Go to **58**.

43

As you get to 'This old man, he played mille quingenti', your stomach is rumbling with hunger. There doesn't seem to be much game in this part of the forest, and you decide to eat some of Getafix's provisions. Oh, your poor feet! It would be nice if a cart came along. Deep in such thoughts, you meet a peasant with a fork over his shoulder.

● You decide to walk on by yourself. Go to **105**.
● He doesn't have a cart, but you would like some company. Go to **69**.

44

This tent seems to be the paymaster's office. There is a lot of slabwork lying around, and on one of the desks you see a small box labelled ENLISTMENT GRATUITIES. You find 20 sestertii in the box; you can add them to your purse. It's a good life in the legions, as the recruiting officers always say!
● You leave the tent.

45

This is a Roman tent like any other, with rows of camp beds and the sheets neatly folded. But you see the corner of a slab sticking out from under a sheet.
● You lift the sheet to find out what is under it. Go to **102**.
● Curiosity is unworthy of you. You leave the tent.

46

The wine is certainly good, but it's strong too. Still, another little sip won't do you any harm . . . and another for the road . . . 'Hey, hand that amphora back!' yells

the Roman. He tries to snatch it from your hands, but falls to the ground, dragging one of the tent poles down with him. The tent collapses. The pair of you are caught like flies in a spider's web. *Take a test of Skill (difficulty 3). But whatever its result, from now until tomorrow morning your points scores for Skill, Fighting Fitness and Charm are each reduced by 3 for drinking too much. Make a note on your Adventure Slab.*
- If you pass, go to **67**.
- If you fail, go to **107**.

47

After your meal, you could really do with a snooze . . . you long for a rest at last!
- You go to sleep on the grass of the clearing, with your sword within reach. Go to **86**.
- You'll be safer up a tree. Climb to **31**.
- You go on, hoping to reach a village soon. Go to **91**.

48

CRASH! The statuette falls to the floor and breaks. The centurion opens first one eye, then the other, and jumps to his feet. Before you can react, he has snatched the gourd and drunk some magic potion from it. He makes for you, shouting, 'Now we'll see if this famous potion really works!'
- You will both find out at **62**.

49

What can you do, a small and not very strong lad from Lutetia, against a beefy patrol of brave legionaries

belonging to the glorious Roman army? You manage to knock out one Roman, maybe two, but the circle closes in again. BOING! Everything goes dark.
- You come round, painfully, at **55**.

50

This must be the cookhouse tent. You see joints of wild boar, vegetables, cauldrons and various cooking utensils. None of it looks very appetising. In fact, it reminds you of your student canteen in Lutetia.
- You make haste to leave this tent.

51

Has the alarm been raised in the camp?
- If it has, go to **90**.
- If not, go to **108**.

52

Phew! One more step and you'd have fallen over a whole heap of weaponry, making enough noise to wake the dead, let alone the Romans.
- You leave the tent.

53

At first sight this tent contains nothing interesting. But then, on the floor, you find a small shield, apparently of Gaulish origin. *You can add the shield to your equipment, and while you are carrying it, it gives you an additional bonus of 5 points on your Fighting Fitness score.*
- You leave the tent.

54

The patrol passes you without stopping. You hear the decurion addressing his men. 'I'll have a spot of like, y'know, order and discipline around here, see? We're going back to camp to report, like, y'know. We'll say we met a band of indomitable Gauls on the Condatum road who outnumbered us, like.'
- When the patrol is out of sight you go on your way to **108**.

55

You come round bound and gagged, inside a yellow tent. You see your bundle, but there is no sign of your gourd of magic potion or your sword (if you had one). *Remember to take these items off your Adventure Slab.*
● Go to **33**.

56

This is a tent like any other, containing camp beds and a small piece of furniture for the legionaries' regulation equipment.
● You decide to waste no time here, and leave the tent at once.
● Or you might decide to look inside the piece of furniture instead. Go to **103**.

57

You leave the tent, but the legionary follows you, shouting jovially, 'Hey, Gaul, let's have another little drink. Long live Culius Jaesar! Hooray for Gaul and the ladies of Lutetia!'

● You are out of the tent and on your way, but all that noise has raised the alarm.

58

Closing the cupboard again, you cause a draught which blows on the centurion's face. Luckily Arteriosclerosus does not wake up. He just grunts and buries his head in the cushions. Where are you going to look now?

● On the table . . . go to **37**.
● In the chest . . . go to **87**.

59

CRASH! What a fall! Athletic as you are, it was still silly to go to sleep in a tree. Better lie on the ground, where you don't risk breaking your neck. Now you're covered with bruises. *Subtract 2 points from your Charm.*
● In spite of the pain you manage to get to sleep. You ought to wake up less suddenly next time, at **86**.

60

'I hope for your sake you're telling the truth, Gaul,' says the centurion. 'Decurion Flebitus, send a messenger to the Prefect of Lutetia. We'll work this lad over a bit anyway, just to check what he says. See you soon, Gaul!'
● Go to **89**.

61

This round tent belongs to the centurion. Putting your head through the tent-flap, you recognise Centurion Arteriosclerosus lying on a couch, half-asleep. You slip inside the tent. The centurion turns over and buries his head in a cushion. He hasn't woken up . . . this is the perfect moment to get your magic potion back. But where is it?
● In the cupboard? Go to **75**.
● In the chest? Go to **87**.
● On the table? Go to **37**.

62

The mists of unconsciousness disperse. You are back in the same tent again, but this time your bonds are VERY tight, and you haven't a hope of escaping. Your father Doublehelix will have to pull strings to get you set free. No doubt he can do it . . . but you'll have to possess your soul in patience, because now YOUR ADVENTURE IS OVER.

63

At every sip the wine tastes better and better. This vintage is real nectar! The Roman army has its good points after all.

- *If you have chosen a good head for drink as your Secondary Aptitude, go straight to* **74**.
- *If not, throw the dice. If you throw 1, 2 or 3, go to* **74**. *If you throw 4, 5 or 6, go to* **46**.

64

I'LL GET YOU!!

Oh no! The legionary you find in here was leader of the patrol that captured you this morning. Recognising you, he makes straight for you. Are you ready to fight back? *His Fighting Fitness score is 18.*

- If you win the fight, you leave the tent.
- If the legionary wins, go to **62**.

65

Sitting comfortably on a mossy stone, you unpack Getafix's provisions. You find smoked meat, some apples, a gourd of cider, rye bread . . . barbarians they may be, but your country cousins certainly eat well!
- Go to **47**.

66

The Romans fall on you, seize your bundle and your gourd of magic potion, and soon you are bound and gagged and being carried along slung from a pilum like a captured boar. After several hours' marching, you arrive at the camp of Totorum still trussed up. The patrol puts you down in a red tent, where a Roman, obviously

the centurion commanding the camp, is lying on a couch. The patrol leader reports. 'Well done, legionary!' says

IN PATROLLING THE FOREST LIKE WHAT YOU GAVE US ORDERS FOR, Y'KNOW, CENTURION, SIR, WE PROCEEDED TO FIND THIS HERE INDIVIDUAL WHAT GAVE US AN ACCOUNT OF HIMSELF WHAT WAS NOT AT ALL SATISFACTORY, LIKE!

the centurion. 'Put this spy in the prison tent, take his weapons to the armoury, and I'll keep that gourd of his!' He puts the precious gourd down on a table, and as the legionaries carry you away, you hear him muttering, 'I bet that gourd contains the famous magic potion which gives the Gauls superhuman strength . . . oh, won't Caesar be pleased with you, Voluptuous Arteriosclerosus!' The Romans leave you on the floor of a yellow tent, still bound and gagged, in a very uncomfortable position. They put your bundle in a corner of the tent and then go away, leaving you alone. All is lost! And what about your mission? Are you going to wait here until Asterix and Obelix come and rescue you? Poor Justforkix! Is this the end?
- Go to **33**.

67

Wriggling under the canvas of the tent, you manage to get out and slip away. The legionaries, busy putting the tent up again, have not seen you leave.
- You are out of the tent, but of course the alarm has been raised.

SOUND THE ALARM! EVERYONE TO ARMS!

68

There is nothing in this tent but camp beds.
- You leave it at once.

69

Seeing you, the man turns round. 'Dang me, young feller-me-lad, if it bain't a real pleasure to meet company, by Belenos* it be!' You fall into conversation with him. You tell him about the high life of Lutetia, and he tells you about his prize cauliflowers and carrots. After a while, he asks you where you're going. You tell him:

● 'I'm on my way to see my family in Lutetia.' Go to **41**.
● 'To do some shopping in Condatum.' Go to **81**.
● 'To visit a friend in Aquae Calidae.' Go to **96**.

*A god of the Gauls.

70

The countryside is looking lovely, you will soon see your uncle and your friends Asterix and Obelix again, and you strike up a song you learned from Cacofonix. 'This old man, he played unum . . . he played duo . . .' right on to 'This old man, he played mille quingenti* . . .'

● Go to **43**.

*1,500.

71

SO THAT'S YOUR LINE, EH?

'We'll leave you to think it over, Gaul. I hope you appreciate our clemency! You should be in a better frame of mind tomorrow. I'd be sorry to have to resort to violent measures unworthy of the glorious Roman army.'

● Go to **89**.

72

Three legionaries attack you at once. This lot must just have arrived from Rome! *They each have a Fighting Fitness score of 18.*

● If you win the fight, you leave the tent.
● If you lose, go to **62**.

73

Entering this big green tent, you find it is like a vast lumber-room. It is full of stuff: spears, swords, dented or incomplete breastplates, vases, cauldrons and other items, probably looted. You think you spot the sword Geriatrix lent you, lying on a table. Yes, that's it all right, rather worn but well balanced, and bearing old Gaulish inscriptions. It must have been an antique even at the time of Gergovia. *You can add the sword to your equipment again.* But in your delight, you stumble over a pilum. *Take a test of Skill (difficulty 4).*

● If you succeed, go to **52**.
● If you fail, go to **83**.

74

You pass the amphora back and forth several times. Suddenly the Roman collapses on his camp bed, dead drunk. He makes a frightful noise about it. Footsteps approach. The noise of his fall must have raised the alarm. You have already taken your courage in one hand and your gourd of potion in the other when a legionary outsider calls, 'Don't worry, it's only old Vinus had a drop too much again! No cause for alarm.'

● Phew! The footsteps retreat, and you leave the tent.

75

Quietly, you open the cupboard and cast a glance at its contents. Togas, weapons, seaside souvenirs, tunics, various knick-knacks, an Egyptian statuette brought back from Caesar's campaigns, but no gourd of potion.

● However, the statuette is very attractive, and covered in gold leaf. It would make a good present for a girl-friend in Lutetia . . . or you might give it to your father.

A present from Egypt . . . it would look good on his desk. You take it with you. Go to **104**.

● What's the point of lumbering yourself with useless objects? No Egyptian idol is going to help you find your uncle. You decide you'd better go in search of the magic potion. Go to **58**.

76

Oops! You scuttle behind a tree and fling yourself on the ground among some dead leaves. No one would know the sun had been shining for the last two days! The ground's really damp. That's the Armorican climate – very bracing, as Obelix would say. But the patrol passes by without spotting you. Belenos is with you.

● Go to **108**.

77

'Is that you, Hippopotamus?' asks the sick legionary. 'Nice of you to come and see me. How about a spot of latruncularius*?' 'Er . . . no, thanks,' you reply, disguising your voice. 'Can't stop – I'm wanted outside.' Is the legionary taken in? *Throw the dice or use the Chance Board.*

● *If you throw 1, 2 or 3,* he thinks it's his friend speaking, and you leave the tent without any trouble.

● *If you throw 4 or more,* go to **85**.

*Not something medical, but a Roman game like draughts.

78

There are ten or so camp beds lined up inside this tent. Searching about a bit, you find a Gaulish sword. You can take it with you if you like . . . though Geriatrix would much rather you brought back his own sword, the antique weapon which fought at Gergovia.

● You leave the tent.

79

Casting a glance around the empty tent, you find a coil of what looks like good stout rope on one of the legionaries' beds. *You can take it with you if you like. Add the coil of rope to your list of Objects.*

● You leave the tent.

80

Good old Getafix! Within a few minutes you've knocked out a whole Roman patrol. Amazing, isn't it?

● In cheerful mood, you set off again, singing. Go to **70**.

81

'Ooh arrgh, oi do know Condatum well. Oi often goes to Condatum for the cattle market. Best of luck, young feller-me-lad. Oi be just off to work in this here field of mine.'

● You go on your way towards Condatum. Go to **108**.

82

There is nothing of any interest in this tent.
● You leave the tent.

83

BIFF!
CRAAAAASH!
!
BOING!
PAF!

How stupid of you! Everything goes crashing to the ground, with a noise like thunder. It must have roused half the camp. Discretion is not your strong point.
● You leave the tent – but the alarm has been raised.

84

'Well, Gaul, I hope for your own sake you're telling the truth,' says the centurion. 'Decurion Flebitus, send a messenger to Centurion Somniferus, commanding the garrison of Aquae Calidae. Tell them to get hold of that Gaulish chief and then all Gaul will be occupied . . . and I mean ALL! None too soon either! Caesar's been going on about that little village for donkey's years! Meanwhile, we'll keep this lad here.'
● Go to **89**

85

'Hey,' cries the legionary, turning his head, 'you're not Hippopotamus!' And summoning up what remains of his strength, he jumps out of bed and is about to call the guard and denounce you as an impostor.
● There's nothing for it: you must attack him! Go to **88**.

86

'Don't move, Gaul!' You are rudely awakened. No, unfortunately it's not a nightmare. You really are surrounded by ten Roman legionaries leaning over you, each one ready to overpower you at the slightest move you make.
● You try to take a dose of magic potion before they have time to do anything. *Take a test of Skill (difficulty 5).* If you fail it, go to **99**. If you pass it, go to **80**.
● You let your enemies capture you, but you are planning to turn the tables. Go to **66**.
● You bravely fight the Roman soldiers without magic potion. Go to **49**.

87

SQUEEEEAAAL

The squeal of the chest's hinged lid as you open it wakes Arteriosclerosus. He sees you and raises himself on one elbow, shouting for the guard. His arm reaches out towards . . . yes, towards your gourd of magic potion lying on the table. You instinctively try diving for it first. *Take a test of Skill (difficulty 4.)*
● If you succeed, go to **34**.
● If you fail, go to **93**.

88

Weak and unarmed, the legionary can't fight very well. *His Fighting Fitness score is only 8 points.*
- If you win the fight, you leave the tent.
- If not, go to **62**.

89

You are left alone in the prison tent, trussed up like a boar ready for the spit. In the evening a legionary comes in with a bowl of lumpy porridge. Next morning he brings you a bowl of milk. You now burst into tears, begging your jailer to loosen your bonds just a little. And he does! After many hours of effort and much contortionism, you manage to free your hands. After that, removing your gag and untying your legs is child's play. And now you must try to get your equipment back. Well, your bundle and your purse aren't far away, but what about your sword, not to mention the magic potion? Enough time's been wasted. At all costs you must get the sword and the potion back and leave the camp as fast as possible.

On the plan of the camp of Totorum opposite, you start from the yellow prison tent. The other tents have numbers on them.

THE MOVES

- Moving from square to square, you can enter a tent from any direction except diagonally. When you enter one, go to the paragraph whose number is shown on it and follow the instructions. You can leave the tent in any direction you like. Then go on moving on the plan.

- You can go into the same tent twice. Any Romans already knocked out will be lying in a corner, unable to fight any more. And any objects you might find there will still be in place.

- When you meet a legionary in any square you must fight him. If you win, cross him out of that square; you can now move through it without a fight.

- When you manage to leave the camp of Totorum by either gate, go to **51**.

THE ALARM

- The first time you fight a legionary outside a tent the alarm will be raised in the tent.

- For the time the alarm has been raised until you leave the camp, you cannot enter a square next to a square containing a legionary without being attacked by him. He then moves to your square, when the fight takes place.

- Each legionary in the camp of Totorum has a Fighting Fitness score of 18 points. You will not get back all your own Fighting Fitness points until you leave the camp. If you lose a fight inside the camp, go to **62**.

THE MAGIC POTION

- If you get your gourd of magic potion back you can use it at once. Once you have drunk a dose of potion, mark a cross on a corner of your Adventure Slab (1) for each fight with a legionary and (2) for each move from one square to another. After the twelfth cross the effects of the potion will wear off. If you meet any more legionaries you will have to take another dose of potion, or fight without potion.

90

You set off for Condatum. The sky is blue, the sun is shining, but there is one big cloud on your horizon; the Romans must be hot on your heels. And speak of the devil . . . here comes a patrol!

● You dive into the shelter of the trees by the roadside to hide. *Take a test of Skill (difficulty 3)*. If you pass, go to **76**. If you fail, go to **36**.

● You carry on along the road whistling, hands in your trouser pockets. Go to **54**.

● Attack is the best form of defence! You take a dose of potion and charge the legionaries. Go to **40**.

91

Night has fallen, and you haven't found a village or an inn yet. Worn out, you slow down, and you end up at a standstill in the middle of the forest.

● You lie down in the ditch by the roadside. Go to **86**.

● Making one last effort, you climb a tree to be in greater safety. Go to **31**.

92

You raise the amphora to your lips and drink deeply, expecting it to be very ordinary Gaulish wine. You get a nice surprise – it's a fine Lusitanian vintage. The Roman takes back his amphora, drinks greedily and hands it back to you, remarking philosophically, 'In vino veritas.'

● You drink a second time. Go to **63**.

● You politely refuse and try to slip away. Go to **57**.

93

As if in slow motion, you see the centurion's hand come down on the gourd a split second before your own. He immediately takes a good gulp, gets to his feet - and punches you on the chin. BOING! You go flying through the air, right out of the tent, you see the sky above, sail over several other tents, and fall heavily to the ground.

● Go to **62**.

94

There are a lot of them, and you are now very weak. How stupid to have escaped from the camp, only to be recaptured a few hours later! BOOM! You are knocked on the head . . .

● You come back to your senses at **62**.

95

Soon after you track down a young wild boar, not much bigger than a piglet, and roast it over your camp-fire.

● Go to **47**.

96

'Oi bain't never heard tell of that there place,' says the man. You explain that it's up in the mountains.

● Your ways part at the next crossroads. You yourself go on to **108**.

97

This must be where the torturer plies his trade. All his instruments are there around a brazier: pincers, tongs, iron bars, even chicken feathers.

● You've seen enough and you leave the tent in a hurry.

98

> HI THERE! HIC! HAEC! HOC!

The legionary doesn't seem to mind having a young Gaul at large in the camp; he's drunk! What is the Roman army coming to?

● You leave the tent.

99

BOING! A Roman unceremoniously brings the flat of his sword-blade down on your skull.
- You wake up again at **55**.

100

Oops! You nearly fell! Two large branches make a safer sort of bed. Now you can sleep soundly.
- Woken by the first rays of the sun, you climb down from your perch and go to **70**.

101

Sure enough, it's nothing but an old caliga. You're out of luck . . . and your back aches from bending. *You lose 3 points each for Fighting Fitness and Skill until you have left the camp.*
- You leave the tent.

102

The slab has a cartoon of Caesar and Cleopatra engraved on it. The artist is quite good. The legionary who sleeps in this bed ought to be grateful to you . . . suppose the centurion had found that slab in his possession! *If you like you can take the slab with you and add it to your equipment.*
- You leave the tent.

103

Well, what did you expect? Treasure? A cauldron full of magic potion? There is nothing but a few legionaries' tunics, a broken sword, an old caliga, a letter from a Roman matron and a lot of useless knick-knacks.
- You leave the tent.

104

Phew! The statuette is heavier than you thought. It slips out of your hands . . .
Take a test of Skill (difficulty 4).
- If you pass, go to **42**.
- If you fail, go to **48**.

105

The merry peasant greets you, in jovial mood. He tries to strike up a conversation with you, but seeing you don't want to talk, he gives up.
- He goes off, and you go on along the road. Go to **108**.

106

There is a Roman soldier lying on one of the camp beds. He is thin, with a pale, spotty face, and he doesn't look very well.
- Are you going to fight him? Suppose he's got something infectious? Go to **88** to find out.
- You try to slip past him. *Take a test of Skill (difficulty 4).* If you pass, you leave the tent. If not, go to **77**.

107

Caught up in the folds of canvas, you struggle as hard as you can, but you can't get free. There are already a number of legionaries busy putting the tent up again. When you finally get your head free, you find you are facing a dozen armed Roman soldiers. Obviously your struggles under the canvas didn't pass unnoticed! Well, never mind, if you have to fight you'll fight! But as you try to stand up you catch your feet in a fold of canvas and fall heavily to the ground again, half stunned. The legionaries instantly throw themselves on you and tie you up.
- Go to **62**.

CHAPTER III

PITFALLS ON THE WAY

108

Worn out, you arrive at Condatum early in the evening. These barbarians call it a town? It's nothing but a big village. Lutetia is the only town in Gaul worth speaking of. But never mind that – where will you stay tonight?
- At the Happy Boar. Go to **127**.
- At the Armorican Pancake. Go to **155**.

109

If you'd only listened to your father and avoided gambling games. Really, you're hopeless! The innkeeper is firm about it: you stay there washing dishes and doing housework until you've paid off your debt.
- You set to work without complaining. Go to **123**.
- Cross, and muttering darkly about wretched country bumpkins, you break half the plates on purpose and make apple-pie beds for the customers. Go to **152**.

110

The usual introductions are made, and you learn that the Gaul's name is Candlewix and his wife is called Taffeta. They are in the textiles business, and have come from Lugdunum for the great annual fair of Condatum which takes place in a week's time. So they know the road you will be travelling tomorrow, and they tell you about their own adventures. They were attacked by brigands while sleeping in their chariot outside a big inn last night . . . is it worth economising?

- You go to the legionaries' table at **138** (unless you have been there already).
- You ask the innkeeper for a room. Go to **171**.
- You try to start a conversation with his daughter at **129** (but don't insist on it if it is not your first attempt).

111

'Get out this minute, or I'll tell the Roman soldiers in the next village we come to! I don't give lifts to passengers in this cart.' And when you stay put, the driver brings his oxen to a halt, rises and rolls his sleeves up. He isn't joking. 'I'll teach you manners, my lad! Get out at once or I punch you on the nose.'
- No point in standing your ground if that's how he feels. You get out of the cart without further objection and carry on on foot. Perhaps the driver of the next cart will be better disposed. Go to **120**.
- You absolutely must get to Aquae Calidae as soon as possible. You fight this curmudgeonly Gaul. It's his own fault – he was asking for it! But he's a hefty specimen . . . *his Fighting Fitness score is 20*. If you win the fight, go to **130**. If you lose, go to **148**.

112

There is a big service station and chariotel* built at the junction with Roman Road X from Lutetia to Burdigala. Exactly what you need. However, if you prefer, or if your finances won't stretch to a night at the inn, you can sleep in the open.
- You go into the inn, at **173**.
- You sleep on the grass outside. Go to **126**.
- You try to sleep in your chariot. Go to **136**.

*Roman motel.

113

Their eyes are shining in the dark. You break out in a cold sweat. But the wolves, frightened by the fire and the movement of your torch, have stopped advancing. Some of them are even retreating towards the wood, while remaining alert. Be brave – you can't go to sleep now; you must go on holding them at bay. The horses' teeth are chattering too! When the first torch begins to burn low, you light a second, and then a third. After what seems like eternity, the sun rises above the trees. The pack of wolves scatters and goes back into the mountains.
- You haven't had much sleep, but you must set off again. Go to **139**.

114

You get the idea. The merchant is trying to palm you off with his wooden chariot, but it would be sensible to buy the copper model instead – that is, if you can afford it!
- Go to **174** to make your choice.

115

The road, narrower and less crowded now, winds its way through fields of wheat and barley. The day passes without incident, but it's a long journey. At last you see the first hills! No sign of any inn, though. These minor roads have very few facilities! You stop your chariot on the outskirts of a little wood and decide to spend the night there. The horses will need a breather before starting to climb the mountain road, and you are beginning to feel tired too after your long journey. You have had enough of Getafix's provisions, and decide to go hunting in the wood. *Take a test of Skill (difficulty 4).*
- If you succeed, go to **134**.
- If you fail, go to **169**.
- *If you have chosen hunting as your Secondary Aptitude*, go straight to **134** *without throwing the dice.*

116

You take the Lugdunum road, a small and recently built Roman road. These Romans are crazy! Fancy building a road which doesn't lead to Lutetia! You drive along at a spanking pace. There are not many people or vehicles about: a few peasants on foot, an occasional ox cart, a few Gothic or Batavian barbarians, and of course the inevitable Roman patrols controlling the traffic. Not an inn in sight. Towards noon you stop to let the horses graze, and you lunch on a few sandwiches from your bundle.
- You go on your way again, to **182**.

117

Coming round in the main room of the inn, you hear a pitiful yell. It turns out to be your own voice yelling! A frightful pain shoots through you. You fall back on the straw mattress which you find underneath you. You must be delirious, you're seeing things – for instance, you see a menhir in one corner of the room. But it's real! Yes, there are your friends. Asterix leans over you. 'Well, Justforkix, what a surprise!' he says. 'What are you doing here? We'd have expected to see you in the

village if anywhere. You're in a bad way, aren't you? It's not a good idea to sleep out of doors, you know; there are brigands everywhere.' 'Mosquitoes too,' says someone else. 'Brigands aren't really bothersome – they don't sting. Mosquitoes sting.' That can only be Obelix speaking. You are just strong enough to tell your friends the whole story. 'Ah,' says Asterix. 'Then we'd better go and tell Vitalstatistix – we left him in Aquae Calidae. His treatment was over and he was planning a nice gastronomic tour of the best restaurants in the town. But Obelix wanted to see his cousin Metallurgix* again, so we thought we'd leave a little earlier and go home by way of Lutetia. That's how we came to be here tonight. Vitalstatistix must have forgotten about his meeting with Chief Whosemoralsar elastix! Thanks for warning us. We'll take over now and complete the mission. Considering the state you're in, I think you'd better stay in bed here and wait for us. We'll pick you up on our way back.' YOUR ADVENTURE IS OVER.

*see ASTERIX AND THE GOLDEN SICKLE.

118

Other friends of his armed with ENORMOUS clubs come to the rescue. There is no hope of escape.
- You take a dose of magic potion. Go to **163**.
- You decide to save your potion. Go to **137**.

119

Calming down, the Roman soldiers take the money and leave the inn. As they go out, one of them tells you, 'You got off lightly this time, but don't let us catch you cheating over again!' Feeling relieved, you apologise to the

innkeeper for this little incident, pointing out that in fact you never cheat (well, almost never), and then:
- You go to the table where the two Gauls are sitting (if you haven't been there already). Go to **110**.
- You ask the innkeeper for a room. Go to **171**.
- You try to get into conversation with his daughter. (Of course, it wouldn't be a good idea to persist if she's already given you the brush-off, particularly after what's just happened.) Go to **129**.

120

Not a chariot on the horizon! On the other hand, if you were going the other way, you could take your pick. Just as you are preparing to rest by the roadside, however, you hear horses' hooves behind you. Eight of them, nicely oiled. It is a little sports chariot. You stick your thumb out, and the chariot slows down and stops. 'Well, young man, where are you going?' asks the charioteer, in a strong Lutetian accent. 'Aquae Calidae? I can drop you off there if you like.' You get into the back of the chariot, a fast model not intended to carry passengers, so you are very uncomfortable. And the charioteer, no doubt to impress you, is urging his horses on at top speed. In fact, he drives just the way you drive yourself! Your stomach heaves – but finally you both arrive at Aquae Calidae safe and sound. Your new friend drops you off at the town gates and goes on his way towards Gergovia.
- Go to **185**.

121

She shows you a small and very simply furnished room. You manage to exchange a quick kiss and a few vague promises with her. Then you lie down on the bed, fall asleep, and have sweet dreams.
- You wake up at **140**.

122

You can't go on with your journey in these circumstances. How stupid you were to gamble your money away! Asterix and Obelix would never have risked their funds on such an important mission. Feeling very annoyed with yourself, you turn back, wondering how

to explain your financial difficulties to Getafix. He'll hand the mission over to someone else, and you will be in disgrace! Poor Justforkix – you may do better another time, but for now, YOUR ADVENTURE IS OVER.

123

'Well, you're not a bad lad at heart,' says the innkeeper, before you leave, 'but you're a rotten gambler. However, you've worked hard, and I can see you've got problems. So here are 30 sestertii to help you get home again. You can pay them back next time you're passing this way.' You don't know how to express your gratitude. You go off into the streets of Condatum, thanking Belenos, Toutatis, Belisama and all the other Gaulish gods for letting you meet such a generous soul.
● Go to **153**.

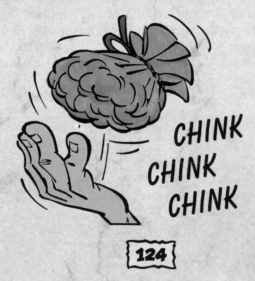

CHINK
CHINK
CHINK

124

Even before daybreak, the Gothic charioteers in the next room are getting up and making a great deal of noise about it. What a way to behave! Fancy waking their fellow guests up like that! Eventually you all three go downstairs, and Asterix pays the bill. 'Well, our ways part here, Justforkix,' he says. 'We'll carry on to Lutetia, and you go to Aquae Calidae. I hope you find our chief in time. If you think you may not have enough sestertii on you for the rest of your journey, we can lend you a few.'
● A few sestertii might well come in handy, and you accept Asterix's offer. Go to **172**.
● 'No, really . . .' You refuse politely. Go to **160**.

125

SCREEECH! The chariot brakes as the horses' hooves scrape on the ground; the poor creatures have difficulty in stopping within such a short distance. The chariot finally comes to a standstill in a great cloud of dust. You have hardly set foot on the ground when four brigands

emerge from the forest. One of them, a hefty fellow armed with a club stuck with nails, comes up to you. 'Don't worry, my lad,' he says. 'No harm will come to you if you hand over all your money.'
● Without turning a hair, you give them your purse (all the more willingly if it happens to be empty). Go to **170**.
● 'I'll show you what a Lutetian's made of, you loudmouth!' Go to **118**.

126

After your snack, you could do with a good night's rest. It is cool, the ground is hard, and you are feeling increasingly sorry you ever started out on this dangerous adventure when you could have stayed in Lutetia, having fun in the taverns of the Latin Quarter. In the middle of the night a slight noise wakes you. Rubbing your eyes, you see a man surreptitiously trying to lead your horses away. You jump up, shouting, 'Stop thief! My chariot!' Caught in the act, the man draws his sword and attacks you. *His Fighting Fitness score is 24.*
● *When the thief's Fighting Fitness score falls below 6,* go to **161**.
● If you lose the fight first, go to **117**.

127

Sitting at your table, you look around you. There are not many customers: some Roman soldiers getting rather merry, and a couple of Gaulish merchants. You're fed up with sandwiches! You're going to treat yourself to a proper meal. The innkeeper, a jovial soul, comes over and suggests one of his specialities:

- Boar in cream sauce. Go to **168**.
- Roast boar with garlic. Go to **147**.
- Boar with mushrooms. Go to **181**.

128

Mecanix offers you 20 sestertii. This is ridiculously low. You must haggle over the price. *To do so, you throw the dice. When you throw 4 or a lower number, you put the price up by 5 sestertii for each throw. As soon as you throw a 5 or a 6, the bargaining is over. You sell your chariot at whatever price you have reached. If you chose business skills as your Secondary Aptitude, don't count the first throw of 5 or 6, but throw the dice again instead.*

- Having added the proceeds of this sale to your purse, you enter the town at **185**.

129

Going up to the girl, you give her your most charming smile. 'That boar was delicious – even better than they cook it in the inns of Lutetia. I wish I could stay longer in this town, but perhaps we'll meet again some other time. Do you ever go to Lutetia?'

- You've been eating roast boar flavoured with garlic. Go to **162**.
- You chose a more delicately flavoured dish. *Take a test of Charm (difficulty 3).* If you pass, go to **149**. If you don't, go to **162**.

130

Having knocked the driver out, you bind and gag him. There's no point in asking for trouble with a patrol of Roman soldiers. Without more ado, you hide the man at the back of the cart behind his hay. You take the reins and drive on along the road to Aquae Calidae. You can imagine yourself telling your friends in Lutetia about your simple and effective methods of hitch-hiking.

- You go on to **164**.

131

The game consists of throwing darts at the board, trying to hit the bull's-eye at the centre. The sailors are playing for money. Each man bets 5 sestertii on each round of the game. If you decide to join in, here's the way to play: like the sailors, you bet 5 sestertii on each round. If you win it, you get back your own stake and the money your four opponents were staking (20 sestertii). If you don't, you lose your stake, and the winners each throw another dart to decide who gets it. You can drop out of the game whenever you like.

Throw the dice once for each of the four sailors. The number you throw shows where your opponent's dart lands. Then take a pencil, hold your hand 50cm above the page opposite, and let the pencil drop, trying to hit the

bull's-eye. If you are still under the influence of the wine you drank in the fortified camp of Totorum, add 20cm to the distance. The mark the pencil makes on the dartboard shows where your dart has landed. If you do not want to spoil the page, or if your pencil doesn't make an obvious enough mark, you could drop a small coin instead. If you are playing in a bus or a train in the rush hour, you can use a dice, like the sailors. Or you can think of other ways to play – the main thing is to win.

● When you have won more than 50 sestertii at darts, go to **179.**

● If you decide to drop out first, or if you don't want to play the game at all, you ask the innkeeper for a room. Go to **171.**

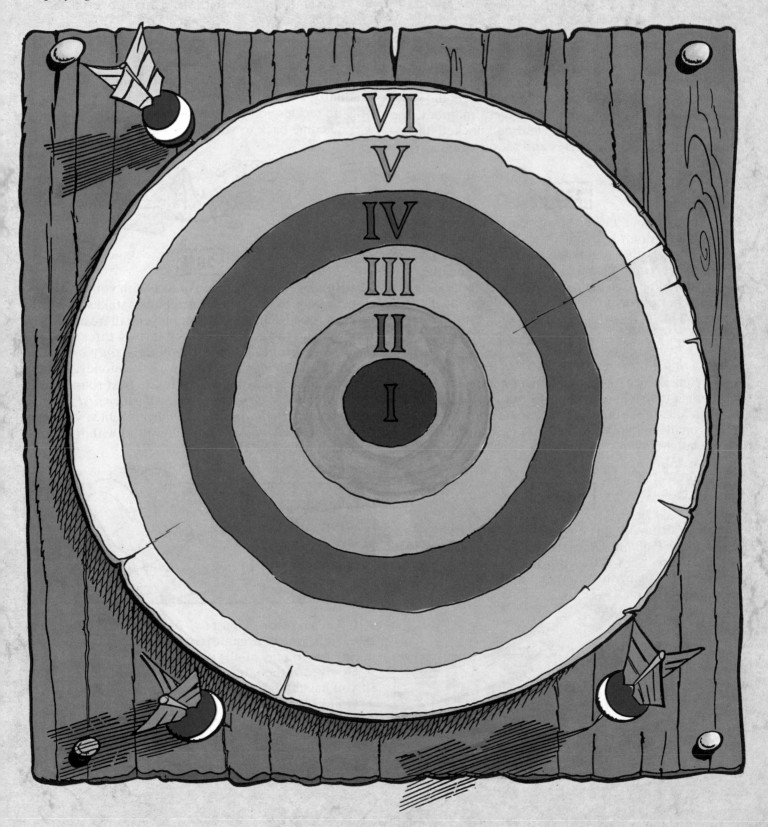

132

YELP! YELP!

Amazing! You never cease to wonder at the effects of the magic potion! Catching a wolf by the tail, you whirl it around in the air and hit its friends with it. When you have worn out this improvised weapon, you throw it into the forest and catch another wolf, which gets the same treatment. After a few minutes of these methods, the wolves are all lying about the clearing knocked unconscious. You soothe the horses and set off again.
• Go to **139**.

133

Even though your father has given you a magnificent Ferrarix, you don't know much about the way a chariot works. On the other hand, you know a good horse when you see one. You notice that the horses pulling the copper chariot look young and fit, whereas those pulling the wooden chariot seem to be elderly and may be ill.
• Go to **174**.

134

Yum, yum! A nice tender wild boar piglet! Let's hope its mother isn't anywhere around, because she might upset your meal, if not your digestion. You cook your catch over a small wood fire, tie up the horses, and go to sleep by moonlight.
• Go to **151**.

135

The three Romans fall on you, shouting. *As they are drunk, their Fighting Fitness is only 10 points each, 30 in all.* The innkeeper watches the brawl in alarm, and then intervenes to calm the combatants down – and avoid damage to his inn.
• If you win, go to **166**.
• If not, go to **184**.

136

Chariots are not meant for lying down in. If only you had your father Doublehelix's fine chariot here instead – the one with the seats that fold down to make a bed! However, this isn't Lutetia.
• You get annoyed, give up, and go into the inn at **173**.
• You count wild boar until sleep finally overtakes you. Go to **178**.

137

Though entirely surrounded, you fight bravely. But gradually exhaustion gets the better of you, and a brigand tackles you and knocks you out.
• You come back to your senses at **154**.

138

The Romans suggest a game of dice with you. There are three rounds to the game. Each player stakes 5 sestertii on each round. Thus, with four players, there are 20 sestertii on the table. Each player throws three dice (*or throws the dice three times if you have only one*), and whoever gets the highest score wins the money. If there is a draw, the stakes are added to the next round of the game. *If you decide to play, throw the dice first for each Roman soldier and finally for yourself.* Once you have begun this game you are not allowed to withdraw until you have played all three rounds.

• If you have won at least two of the three rounds, go to **180**. If not, when the game is over (or straight away if you decide not to play at all) you can:
• Go over to the table where the two Gauls are sitting (if you haven't been there already). Go to **110**.
• Go to **171** and ask the innkeeper for a room.
• Go to **129** and strike up a conversation with his daughter. (But don't insist on it if you've tried that already; it would make you look rude, and wouldn't be worthy of the son of a distinguished Lutetian family.)

139

Sleeping outside is not all it's cracked up to be! Time to be off again! The road climbs now, the horses are straining, but you will soon be up in the mountains. At last Aquae Calidae comes in sight – the horses are done for. As you enter the town, you notice a sign saying MECANIX: USED CHARIOTS.
- You try to resell your chariot, you could do with the money and it won't be very useful here. Go to **128**.
- You decide to hang on to it. Go to **185**.

140

You come downstairs early next morning. Breakfast is delicious: goat's milk and pancakes. But your bill adds up to 10 sestertii (5 for your room, 5 for breakfast).
- You pay your bill and leave the inn. Go to **153**.
- By Toutatis! There aren't enough sestertii left in your purse to pay the bill! Where have all those sestertii gone? Go to **109**.

141

The Romans rise unsteadily to their feet and come towards you. They have drunk even more than you thought! 'Thief! Cheat!' they accuse you. 'You don't wriggle out of it that way! Give us our sestertii back!'
- No point in arguing, they might bring the whole garrison down on you. You return all the money you've won since the start of the game. Go to **119**.
- You're not going to let them do you out of your honest gains. Go to **135**.

142

This chariot goes all right, though it's rather heavy and hard to manoeuvre. You daren't drive it like your own lovely sports chariot . . . well, no good crying over spilt milk! Driving an old banger like this may be beneath you, but still, it should get you to Aquae Calidae. *When you take a test of Skill while driving this chariot, the difficulty factor will be 4.*
- Drive on to **116**.

143

In the pale moonlight, you make out a dark shape moving on the outskirts of the wood, and then another a little farther off. Suddenly these shapes stand out more clearly against the dark background . . . help! Wolves! One of them utters a howl which freezes your blood. You look behind you. You are surrounded!

- Horrible brutes! You take a dose of magic potion and then attack them. Go to **132**.
- Luckily, there is a tree for you to climb. You go up it like greased lightning. Go to **157**.

144

By Toutatis, what hopeless horses! They don't understand a thing. They turn right when you want to go left, and they start galloping when you want them to stop. And as the axle sags at the slightest provocation, the chariot pitches dangerously when you take a bend. Now you know why it was so cheap. But despite your bad luck, you don't lose heart. You leave Condatum, hoping this chariot will at least get you to Aquae Calidae. *When you take a test of Skill while driving this chariot, the difficulty factor will be 5.*
- You go to **116**.

145

The Gaulish countryside isn't safe these days. First brigands attacking you, now someone trying to steal your chariot . . . crime's as bad here as in Lutetia. Though at least there are legionaries on every street corner in Lutetia. But of course, you're doing your best to avoid legionaries at the moment. Perhaps the countryside has its good points after all!

● Thinking along these lines, you go to sleep again, in your chariot this time so as to forestall any further attempts to steal it. Go to **183**.

● There's still time to go to the inn at **173**, as you should have done straight off.

146

The brigands disappear into the forest, and after your first stunned reaction, you take stock of all the difficulties facing you. No money, no transport - all you can do is hitch-hike back to the village. You're a feeble, hopeless coward! Getafix made a big mistake when he entrusted this mission to you. YOUR ADVENTURE IS OVER.

147

The innkeeper's daughter brings you your boar and a bowl of cider. The boar is a little overcooked for your liking and there's rather too much garlic in it . . . you think nostalgically of Impedimenta's roast boar! Fussy about your food, aren't you?

● You finish up your boar and go to **156**.

148

The carter chucks you out with a sharp nudge of his elbow. Stunned and aching, you take some time to get to your feet. By the time you are able, with difficulty, to get moving again, the ox cart is well ahead. Limping, you carry on on foot.

● Go to **120**.

149

'Oh, do you live in Lutetia?' she asks. 'Aren't you lucky! I've never been there, but I hope I will some day. It must be a wonderful place!' Once again you realise,

not without pride, that your Lutetian charm and high-class accent get you a lot of admiration in the backwoods here. But your weariness overcomes you, and fore-seeing a long day ahead, you ask the girl to show you your room.

● Go to **121**.

150

Discouraged, head bent, you are walking on along the Roman road when you hear the sound of wheels behind you. An ox cart with a load of hay is jogging along at a steady pace. You wave to the driver and ask him, 'Can

you give me a lift? I'm going to Aquae Calidae.' 'No, I can't, I never give lifts to hitch-hikers,' says the man.

● You go on on foot, hoping for better luck next time. Go to **120**.

● There's no time to be lost: taking no notice of this far from warm welcome you jump up into the hay at the back of the cart. Go to **111**.

151

A blow on the nape of the neck wakes you. But it's only a horse's hoof. Perhaps that's the way the horses show affection for their master . . . NEEIIIGH! You hear the second horse whinnying as it paws the ground. Nervy creatures, aren't they?

● You light a torch (if you have one left, of course). Go to **165**.

● You stay on the look-out in the darkness. Go to **143**.

● You try to get to sleep again. Go to **175**.

152

Next morning you are kicked out of the inn without a sestertius in your pocket. 'And never set foot in my inn again, you scamp!' shouts the innkeeper.

● Feeling ashamed of yourself, you go to **122**.

153

The situation is serious: Vitalstatistix MUST get to that meeting with Chief Whosemoralsarelastix, or the peace of Armorica is in danger. And it will all be your fault too! You can't continue your journey on foot; you need some proper means of transport. In the circumstances, what you want is a chariot. A used chariot dealer in the centre of the town makes you the following offer. 'Here we have a superb light chariot, copper bodywork, a real sports model. I'll let you have it with its two grey horses for 50 sestertii: It's a marvel! And this wooden chariot has two horses too; it's on offer at 40 sestertii. Not so elegant, but it's a good solid model. A real bargain, believe you me!'

● *You chose business skills as your Secondary Aptitude.* Go to **114**.
● *You chose livestock-rearing as your Secondary Aptitude.* Go to **133**.
● *You didn't choose either of those aptitudes.* Go to **174**.

154

You come round again in the forest, alone and badly bruised. Your swollen limbs refuse to move. However, your mind is working fast enough, and you realise with horror that not only have your purse and your bag of provisions been stolen, your gourd of magic potion has gone too. The wreckage of your chariot is still there, but the horses have been taken. Some peasants are moving the tree trunk to let their oxen past. One of them, hearing your groans, finds you and decides to take you to see a druid in the town of Torunes. The druid nurses you for a week, and then sends you home to your family, saying you need a month's convalescence. YOUR ADVENTURE IS OVER. Get well soon.

155

As you open the door of the inn, you nearly get your eye put out by a dart shooting past your shoulder. Four Armorican sailors are absorbed in their game. You sit down at one of the tables and order a meal. The innkeeper brings you a large buckwheat pancake with a small boar covered with cream sauce on top of it. A local speciality, and it's delicious. You must remember to tell Impedimenta about it! After the meal:

● Feeling tired, you ask the innkeeper for a room. Go to **171**.
● Curious about the game, you go over to the darts players. Go to **131**.

156

The Roman soldiers are playing dice. You go over to their table. Go to **138**.

● You would rather talk to the two Gauls. Go to **110**.
● You ask the innkeeper for a room. Go to **171**.
● You strike up a conversation with his pretty daughter. Go to **129**.

157

Well, they do say that fear lends one wings, and you're the living proof of it, perched on a branch. Beads of sweat stand out on your brow, you daren't move, and you watch the carnage below, terrified and powerless. Your horses defend themselves as best they can, but it is a one-sided fight: there are a great many wolves, and they are very hungry. At daybreak, all is silent as the grave; the chariot is no use without horses. But you won't get to Aquae Calidae on foot until tomorrow.

● Go to **150**.

158

You go through the town gates at a gallop, striking panic into the hearts of the guards, and you can't resist slewing your horses round in a showy manner. Luckily it comes off this time. Still, this chariot is nowhere near as good as the Ferrarix your father gave you. *When you are told to take a test of Skill with your chariot, the difficulty factor will be 3.*

● You go to **116**.

159

'Never mind!' says the chariot dealer. 'I've got another little beauty here – you can have it for just 20 sestertii.'

● You have enough money to buy this chariot. You don't really like the look of it, or its horses, but do you have any choice? You pay for it and go to **144**.
● If you don't have 20 sestertii, or if you don't really want to buy the chariot, go to **122**.

160

You part outside the inn. You yourself set off for Aquae Calidae. Just think of Asterix and Obelix trusting you to carry out such a difficult mission! Are you a genuine Gaulish warrior now? At last Vitalstatistix may perhaps feel proud of you.

● Go to **115**.

161

Wounded and exhausted, he runs away without waiting for any more. It is dark, and you can't see a thing; you lose sight of him. All you hear is a horse galloping away: no doubt it has the would-be thief on its back.

● He must be well away by now. Go to **145**.

162

'We never go to Lutetia, and as for looking round Condatum, you'd better ask my father about that. He knows the town much better than I do.' Feeling rather put out, you can:
● Go over to the Roman soldiers' table at **138** (if you haven't been there already).

● Sit down with the Gaulish couple (if you haven't talked to them yet). Go to **110**.
● Go to bed. Go to **171** to ask the innkeeper if he has a room free.

163

The bandits are strong, and there are a lot of them, but Getafix's potion really is magic. After a brief punch-up, you are the only one left on your feet, with a heap of stunned barbarians in front of you. You recover your purse (unless the brigands have already got it). The lingering effects of the potion give you enough strength to clear the road, replant the splendid oak the outlaws knocked down, and straighten out the wheels of your chariot, which are not in very good shape after your emergency stop. When you set off again, night is beginning to fall.

● Go to **112**.

164

By Toutatis, this cart is slow! Ox-carts climb hills well enough, but they've got no acceleration. If only you hadn't crashed your beautiful chariot at the gates of the Gaulish village! You go on for several hours, and then at last – hooray! – you see Aquae Calidae! You leave the cart at the town gates, first untying its owner, who hurls insults at you. You never knew carters had so rich and imaginative a vocabulary!

● You enter the town, feeling optimistic and very sure of finding Uncle Vitalstatistix. Go to **185**.

165

Using your tinderbox, a present from a Lutetian girl-friend, you light one of the torches Getafix gave you. You see shadowy shapes against the outskirts of the wood. At that moment a dreadful sound is heard. HOOOOOWL! Large grey wolves are coming towards you. Rooted to the spot with terror, you can already see yourself being torn to pieces and eaten. You think for the last time of your friends, your family, Lutetia, the Latin Quarter . . . you try to recollect the best moments of your life. No, come on, Justforkix! Be brave, pull yourself together, remember you're a Gaulish warrior!

● You take a dose of magic potion before striding out to meet the wolves. Go to **132**.
● There happens to be a tree right beside you. You'd be out of reach there. You climb it at **157**.
● You wave your torch about to scare the wolves off. Go to **113**.

166

The startled innkeeper sees you knock out the three legionaries with a single blow. Once the fight is over he comes up to you, tearing his hair. 'You're mad!' he says. 'You'll bring the whole patrol down on us. And look at the state you've left my place in!' Then he calms down a bit. 'Well, never mind, considering the state they're in themselves, I shouldn't have any trouble in persuading them that they did all this damage fighting each other. But you can still pay me for the table and chairs you've smashed. That's 50 sestertii worth of damage, that is. And you can go and spend the rest of tonight somewhere else. I don't want any trouble with the Roman army.'
● As you have no choice in the matter, you give the inn-keeper the 50 sestertii you won at dice and leave the inn, grumbling. You decide to try the other inn, the Armorican Pancake. Go to **155**.

167

Surprised to meet this unexpected obstacle, the horses gather themselves and try to jump the tree trunk. One of them catches its hoof in a branch, and you go sailing in the air above the trees. You just have time to see a party of brigands emerge from the forest, and then you come down – PAF! – knocking yourself out.
● You might come round at **154**.

168

The innkeeper's daughter brings you a boar smothered in cream sauce and a bowl of cider. Another local speciality to add to your recipe collection!
● Once the meal is over, go to **156**.

169

What a dear little wild boar piglet! You try to knock it out with a well aimed blow of your fist, just like Obelix. He would be proud of you. HELP! Its furious mother is charging you from behind. The shock of the impact makes you let go of your prey, which scampers off, grunting. Rubbing your behind, you decide not to give chase. You have dropped something on the ground, and you can't find it in the dark. *Choose one item to be removed from your equipment.* You sit down on a rock, making a face, and unwrap a few sandwiches. When you have tied the horses up you go to sleep.
● Go to **151**.

170

'Is that all you've got? Sorry, but we'll just have to take your horses and this chariot!'
● You let them have the horses and the chariot. Go to **146**.
● This is going beyond a joke! Go to **118**.

171

The innkeeper shows you into a very plainly furnished little room. You soon drop off into a dreamless sleep.
• You wake up at **140**.

172

'I'm surprised Getafix didn't give you enough money for your journey,' says Asterix. 'Well, here are 20 sestertii, and mind you don't squander them.'
• You are richer by 20 sestertii, but your pride has suffered. It seems you can't cope on your own! Your morale is lowered for the rest of your journey, and you lose 3 Fighting Fitness points. Go to **160**.

173

A notice points you to the chariot park reserved for the inn's patrons; there is a night watchman. Relieved, you go into the main room of the inn, which contains fifty or so people: Goths, Iberians, Helvetians, and of course Gaulish charioteers and carters. You can hardly hear yourself speak. What a racket! Then you hear a familiar voice. 'Justforkix! What a surprise! Why are you here and not in the village?' It is Asterix waving to you from the back of the room. Obelix is tucking into several wild boar. How glad you are to see your friends again! 'Are you on your way back?' you ask. 'But where's Vitalstatistix? Getafix sent me to find him. He's wanted in the village for a very important meeting!' 'Hi, Justforkix,' says Obelix, putting the last legbone of his boar down. Quickly, you tell them about your adventure. Asterix thoughtfully scratches his head. 'We left Vitalstatistix at Aquae Calidae when his treatment was over,' he says. 'He was about to go on a gastronomic tour of the best inns. And as Obelix wanted to visit his cousin Metallurgix we decided to set off ahead of him and go home by way of Lutetia. That's why we thought we'd spend the night here. Dear me – I'm sure the chief has forgotten all about the meeting. Let's hope your mission finishes as well as it's begun, Justforkix. Would you like us to come with you?'

• Hm . . . it's a dangerous journey, and the company of Asterix and Obelix would be welcome. You accept the suggestion. Go to **177**.
• What do these country bumpkins think you are? You'll show them what a Lutetian can do! You turn down Asterix's offer. Go to **176**.

174

• You decide to buy the copper chariot for 50 sestertii. Go to **158**.
• You economise and resign yourself to buying the wooden chariot for 40 sestertii. Go to **142**.
• You aren't rich enough to buy either. Go to **159**.

175

The animals calm down. You wearily close your eyes, and immediately fall into a deep sleep.
• Go to **151**.

176

'Well, the best of luck, Justforkix!' That's right – you're perfectly capable of coping by yourself! It's getting late when the three of you ask the innkeeper for beds for the night. He puts you all together in a small, stuffy room, saying the rest of the inn is full. 'What can you expect with so much traffic on the roads these days? But of course, if you'd rather, you can always sleep out of doors among brigands and thieves . . . ' 'And mosquitoes,' adds Obelix. 'Brigands aren't so dangerous, they don't sting. Mosquitoes sting.' You all settle down for the night as best you can.
• Go to **124**.

177

'Just as I feared,' says Asterix. 'Really, I can't think why Getafix sent you on this mission. It's too dangerous for you. I think you'd better go back to the village while we go in search of Vitalstatistix. Don't worry, you can go back to Armorica, but YOUR ADVENTURE IS OVER.'

178

You toss and turn, but at last you find a reasonably comfortable position and drop off to sleep.
● You wake up at **183**.

179

The sailors are getting annoyed. One of them throws a dart which buries itself in the door instead of the target. He turns abruptly towards you. 'Don't get too cocky, youngster, or we mightn't like it, by Toutatis!' 'Hold on,

Seasix,' says one of his friends, catching his shoulder. 'I reckon we've played enough for today. You're not on form, that's all! Let's go!'
● The sailors leave the inn, and you go to **171** to ask for a room.

180

The Roman soldiers, who are starting on their third amphora of wine, are giving you some rather nasty looks. When you prudently decide to walk away, one of them suddenly rises to his feet and bangs the table. 'Cheat! I saw him – he was cheating!' And his companions, rather drunk, back him up. 'That's right, he was cheating!' 'Give us our money back, thief!'
● It wouldn't do any good to start a brawl. Restraining your fury, you give them back the money you've won since the game started. Go to **119**.
● You try to reason with them. 'Here, calm down! I didn't cheat, I was in luck, that's all. We'll stop playing and say no more about it.' Go to **141**.
● You're not going to have a bunch of drunken legionaries do you down! Rolling up your sleeves, you ask, 'Who called me a cheat?' Go to **135**.

181

The innkeeper's daughter brings you your boar. It's very good, quite well cooked, but it can't compare with Impedimenta's roast boar.
● When your dinner is over, you go to **156**.

182

As you are driving through a wood, you come round a bend and see a tree trunk lying across the road. To avoid hitting the obstacle, *take a test of Skill. The difficulty factor will depend on the type of chariot you are driving.*
● If you pass, stop in time at **125**.
● If you fail, go flying into the air at **167**.

183

Before sunrise you are woken by the sound of the first ox-carts leaving for Lutetia with their loads. Stiff from sleeping on the hard floor of your chariot, you sit up and eat a bit of bread to give you strength. You don't much like early rising, but it will mean you can get more of the journey behind you today. You set off again to Aquae Calidae in search of your Uncle Vitalstatistix!
● Go to **115**.

184

You come to your senses next morning, lying in bed with a bandage round your head. When you put your hand to your belt . . . YOUR PURSE HAS GONE! Not only have the Roman soldiers taken their 50 sestertii back, they've gone off with the rest of your money too. Luckily you still have the gourd of magic potion!
● Go to **109**.

CHAPTER IV

IN THE ARVERNIAN COUNTRYSIDE

185

A few years ago your father went to Aquae Calidae for a course of treatment. Like Vitalstatistix, he doesn't mind a little banquet now and then – though of course he never overeats. The streets of Aquae Calidae are full of a curious mixture of Gauls, Romans and barbarians. People come here from the ends of the Roman Empire to drink the mineral waters of the springs, breathe the pure air of the Arvernian mountains, and get medical care from top druids. And if what your father says about the place is true, Vitalstatistix can't have been having much fun!

● You can't miss the health farm and hydro run by the druid Diagnostix, situated near the springs, at **207**.

186

Ouff! This window just won't open! And there's not much time – the three centurions are coming closer! Ah, at last! The window flies open. But as you are about to jump out, something hits you over the head.

● You lose consciousness and come round at **208**.

187

'Well, young man, what seems to be the trouble?' asks Diagnostix. 'Listen, I'm not ill!' you say in confidential tones. 'The druid Getafix has sent me to find Chief Vitalstatistix. He's urgently needed at home.' 'Vitalstatistix? Oh dear!' says Diagnostix. 'The fact is, just as he was about to leave us yesterday, a Roman patrol burst

into my consulting rooms and seized him. He couldn't even resist – he was under the shower at the time. And it's all my fault! I forbade him to take any of the magic potion during his treatment. I suspect it of being fattening. Your chief will have been taken to the camp of Axium by now. I'm very, very sorry about what happened here.' But you, Justforkix, know that the druid Diagnostix wasn't really to blame for the capture of

Vitalstatistix. No, it was your own fault! You incautiously let the Romans know where Vitalstatistix was! You can't see the difference between a peasant and a Roman spy! You're liable to tell the first Roman centurion you come across all about your mission! Not only have you failed to complete it, but because of you the chief of the Gaulish village is now a prisoner of the Romans. You'd better give up any ideas of cunning. Rescuing Vitalstatistix would be quite beyond you. You

might well make matters even worse. YOUR ADVEN-
TURE IS OVER. You go home to Lutetia, hoping that
Asterix and Obelix can put things right.

188

Luckily Vitalstatistix has taken a little magic potion.
Without it, you wouldn't hold out against an entire
patrol for long. As it is, however, the Romans are soon
lying about the charcoal in heaps, stunned. Winesanspirix hurries in. 'You'd better get out of here fast, before
any more Romans arrive. I'll tell them I didn't know you
were hiding at my place. They'll think you got in through
the cellar window when you saw a patrol in the street.
Look, here's a map of Gergovia I got from the tourist
bureau. It'll help you find your way out of town. Better
get going quick! See you soon, I hope!'
• You hurry out into the street at **233**.

189

You have terrible nightmares, dreaming of brigands,
Romans, wolves . . . you're certainly having a tiring
journey. At last the night ends. When you wake up,
Winesanspirix is already up and dressed. 'Rise and
shine, friends!' he says. 'I'm going to do a bit of shopping
– I'll drop in on my friend Grocerix and buy you some
sausage, blue Arvernian cheese and rye bread for your
journey. You wait for me here.' You are packing your
things when the front door is suddenly flung open. It's
Winesanspirix back again, out of breath. 'There are

THERE ARE ROMANS
ALL OVER THE PLACE!

Romans all over the place!' he gasps. 'They're con-
fiscating all the wine and all the charcoal and they're
looking for you! Quick, hide! Here they come!' Someone knocks on the door several times. You grab hold of
Vitalstatistix, and the pair of you hide:
• In the charcoal store. Go to **203**.
• In the cellar among the barrels of wine. Go to **211**.

190

There is an old Arvernian behind the counter. Maybe he
knows Vitalstatistix? 'I certainly do!' he tells you. 'We
met in the Gallic War. He lives in Armorica these days,
along with another friend of mine, Geriatrix. He
dropped in to visit me yesterday evening. He's staying
with another veteran of '52, Winesanspirix, who lives
just next door. You're from Armorica too, are you?' At
last you know where your uncle is!
• You leave Localpolitix's shop and go to see his neighbour Winesanspirix at **204**.

191

Three old Arvernians are swapping stories of the Gallic
War. They greet you when you sit down at their table
and carry on with their stories. You listen to them with
half an ear as you enjoy your boar in wine sauce. What a
feast! You'll have some good tales to tell Impedimenta
when you get back – if you get back, that is . . . 'Vercingetorix – now there was a chief for you!' one of the
old men is saying. 'He showed the Romans what was
what, that he did! I remember we were meeting round
at Localpolitix's place one evening – or was it at Geriatrix's . . . ?' 'Geriatrix!' you exclaim. 'Why, I know
someone called Geriatrix, and he was at the siege of
Gergovia! It must be the same man!' They immediately
ask you how the old boy is, tell you about his past
exploits . . . and good manners compel you to listen to
their stories of the Gallic War until the meal is over.
Poor Justforkix! Much, much later you manage to slip
away. You pay for your meal (10 sestertii) and leave.
• You set off for Gergovia at **229**.

192

'Listen, babe, you're a nice lad, but if I knew where
this Superstatistix of yours was I'd have told you,
wouldn't I? I don't poke my nose into other people's
business, but you could ask the boss. He may know.
Ave, handsome!'
• You get her general drift. Go to **220**.

193

A few minutes later the Roman soldiers are lying on the ground, knocked senseless. You go over to Thermostatix, rolling up your sleeves. He caves in at once. 'No, don't! I'll tell all!' he says. 'I informed the Romans when I found out there was someone hiding at Winesanspirix's place.' 'Well, we'll let you go,' says your uncle, 'but you must tell your Roman friends Winesanspirix doesn't know me. And watch your step. If my friend Winesanspirix should happen to be arrested, you might see us again sooner than you bargain for. Now get out!' When the traitor has left, Winesanspirix urges you to get moving too. 'You must be out of here before the other patrols arrive. I'll tell them I didn't know you were hiding at my place. Now, where's my map of Gergovia? Ah, here we are! Take it – it's a slablet produced by the tourist office, and you might find it useful for leaving the town. See you soon!'

- You leave at **233**.

194

OH, YES . . . NOW I REMEMBER!

'Wait a minute. I think it's coming back to me . . . yes, Winesanspirix, that was it. Their friend from Gergovia is called Winesanspirix.'

- You know enough; you leave for Gergovia at **198**.

195

The Roman soldiers, who are rather drunk, have taken a liking to you. After a while they start up an animated and tipsy political discussion. 'Here's to Scipio!' cries one of them, waving his glass about. 'Scipio's a traitor! Long live Julius Caesar!' says a second legionary. 'They're all a rotten lot!' says a third. Suddenly one of the Romans turns to you. 'Hey, Gaul – do you support Scipio – hic! – or Caesar?' You reply:

- 'Caesar.' Go to **226**.
- 'Scipio.' Go to **197**.

- Careful . . . could this be a trap? You'd rather stay neutral. 'I don't know much about politics,' you say. Go to **221**.

196

Have you told them you were going to Aquae Calidae?
- If you have, go to **187**.
- If not, go to **222**.

197

'Quite right, Gaul! Long live Scipio – hic! Down with the usurper – haec, hoc!' says one of the legionaries, collapsing on the table and tipping it over. Fascinated by this edifying spectacle, you have failed to hear three centurions rise and come towards you.

- Go to **215**.

198

Gergovia is only a few milia passuum from Aquae Calidae, so you decide to go there on foot, leaving your chariot behind with Diagnostix (if you still have one). Your horses need to recover from the thrills and spills of the journey. A little walking never hurt anyone, as Vitalstatistix always says when he goes walkabout on his shield in the village. And it will give you a chance to see something of the Arvernian countryside. In a beautiful valley, you see a luxurious-looking inn beside a mountain stream. It is called the Boar in Wine.

- You carry on to **229**, so as to get to Gergovia quickly.
- You stop at this inn to pursue your inquiries, especially as you have what Obelix would describe as a bit of a hole inside you. Go to **227**.

199

Your movement has caused a certain amount of confusion, and the Roman soldiers watching your uncle suddenly turn your way. Vitalstatistix takes his chance to get to his feet and drink some magic potion.
- Go to **193**.

200

'It's no good asking any more questions. We don't keep tabs on our patients after they've left!'
- As you can find out no more, you ask to see the druid Diagnostix. Go to **220**.

201

One of the centurions is about to tie your hands behind your back with a length of cord. Once he's done that it will be too late. You must get to Gergovia to find your uncle, so you will have to escape from the Romans. Do you have any magic potion left?
- If you have, you take a dose. Go to **223**.
- If not, you try running for it. Go to **186**.

202

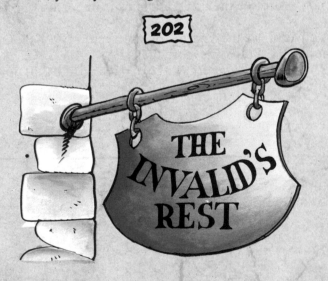

THE INVALID'S REST

This is just the sort of inn Vitalstatistix likes. You go in and ask the innkeeper about him. 'A Gaulish chieftain? Red-haired, rather thin, with pigtails and an Armorican accent? With a couple of other Gauls, a small fair one and a fat one carrying a menhir, right? Yes, I remember it well, they dined here only last week. They talked a lot, specially the fat man. They asked me if I knew a friend of theirs they were planning to visit, an Arvernian restaurant owner who lives in Gergovia. I forget his name.'
- You set off for Gergovia straight away. Go to **198**.
- You go to see what you can find out at the other inn, the Thermal Springs. Go to **213**.
- You slip the innkeeper 10 sestertii, hoping his memory will come back to him. Go to **194**.

203

You both plunge into the middle of the vast pile of charcoal. Suppose your Lutetian friends could see you now! You hear Winesanspirix open the door of his shop. 'We're looking for a dangerous outlaw,' says a Roman voice. 'A Gaulish warrior – a fat little man with red pigtails.' 'Awfully sorry,' says your friend, 'but there's nobody here except me and the wife.' 'Men, search the place!' says the decurion leading the Roman patrol. 'You two go down to the cellar – you three search the charcoal store, and the rest of you go upstairs.'
- This looks serious. Go to **206**.

204

Why, of course you remember what Asterix told you! The helpful Arvernian who gave him and Obelix hospitality while they were in Gergovia was called Winesanspirix. You open the door and hear a familiar voice. Your Uncle Vitalstatistix! His treatment may have helped him lose a bit of weight, but he's not far off his usual size again now. 'What a surprise!' he cries. 'Come here, Justforkix! This is Winesanspirix – we were at the siege of Gergovia together. Why not have a bite to eat with us? Winesanspirix, this is my nephew Justforkix from Lutetia.' 'Lutetia? Really?' says the Arvernian. 'But what are you doing here in Gergovia?' asks your uncle. You put your slablets on the table.* 'By Toutatis!' he exclaims. 'I completely forgot about that meeting!

Ah, well, my duty as chief . . . obligations, protocol and all that . . . someone has to sacrifice himself for the village. One can't think of everything – but thanks to you, nephew, I'll be able to do my duty for my people! We'll leave at dawn.' You seem to have completed your mission. You've found your uncle, and now you can go back to the village with him. Getafix will be proud of you. But don't count your chickens before they're hatched; who knows what may yet happen? Winesanspirix's wife puts an earthenware bowl full of some strange mixture on the table. 'It's good thick Arvernian soup,' Winesanspirix explains. 'We make it with bacon, carrots, turnips, cabbage and sausages.' Worn out after your long journey, you go to sleep over the meal like a little boy. Winesanspirix has to rouse you to get you upstairs to bed. Before calling on him, did you go into Thermostatix's shop?

- If you did, wake up at **232**.
- If you didn't, wake up at **189**.

*Nowadays we would say 'put your cards on the table'.

205

Concentrating on your boar, you are not paying much attention to three Roman centurions sitting at the next table. But when one of them mentions the name Vitalstatistix you prick up your ears. 'That's right, Lotus-eatus, he's here in the Arvernian countryside,' the centurion continues. 'All we have to do is find him, capture him and send him off to Caesar.' 'And there's another thing too, Longtoreignoverus – without him, those indomitable Gauls won't be a thorn in our Roman flesh much longer.' 'But how can we find him, Somniferus?' asks the third centurion. 'There's an awful lot of Arvernian countryside. It'll be easy for him to escape or hide.' 'Ah,' says the first speaker, 'he's sure to go to Gergovia, and we have a good informer there, Thermostatix, an Arvernian shopkeeper. He has a description, and he'll help us pick him up. Let's just hope those two total idiots

commanding the garrison of Gergovia, Centurions Crapulus and Pusillanimus, don't let him escape.'
- There's no need to listen to any more; you've found out enough. You rise from the table, pay for your boar (10 sestertii) and set off for Gergovia. Vitalstatistix is in danger! You must find him and leave these parts. Go to **229**.

206

The cellar doors open, and next moment the Roman soldiers are stirring the charcoal about. BOING! OUCH! A pilum has just hit your head. You hear a legionary shout, 'Quick, here he is, in the charcoal!' His companions rush into the cellar, and like a true warrior you rise to your feet to face them. Vitalstatistix emerges from the heap of charcoal to help you too.
- Even though your uncle is there, you decide to take a dose of magic potion. Go to **230**.
- You bravely fight without potion. Go to **188**.

207

You go into the building pointed out to you, leaving your chariot outside, if you still have it. A secretary meets you. 'Can I help you?' she asks. 'I want to know if my uncle Chief Vitalstatistix is still here,' you say. The secretary consults her filing slabs. 'Sorry, he left us several days ago.' Oh no! It just isn't possible! Where can he gave gone? Hoping for more information:
- You ask to see the druid Diagnostix in person. Go to **220**.
- You turn on the charm for the secretary's benefit. You suspect she knows more than she's letting on. *Take a test of Charm (difficulty 4)*. If you pass, go to **192**. If not, go to **200**.

208

Why are you always getting into such hopeless situations? Here you are again, a prisoner of the Romans, and what's more, behind stout bars. The jailer explains that you're charged with sowing discord among the legionaries, and your trial will take place in a few days time. You're in a nice mess now: no weapons, no magic potion. Poor Justforkix – you shouldn't have gone meddling in other people's business. YOUR ADVENTURE IS OVER. No doubt you'll soon be set free, but it will be too late for you to go in search of Vitalstatistix. May the gods protect him!

209

Did you tell the peasant you met on the way to Condatum that you were going to Aquae Calidae?
• If you did, go to **187**.
• If not, go to **222**.

210

They're completely sozzled! They carry on boozing, and their conduct is lacking in cordiality, to say the least of it. You refusal has annoyed them. You are relieved to hear them start a political discussion. 'Here's to Scipio!' cries

one of them, raising his glass. 'Down with Scipio! Up with Julius Caesar!' another contradicts him. 'They're

all rotten to the core!' says the third. Then, unfortunately, one of them turns to you and asks you your opinion. 'Hey, Gaul – hic! – are you for Caesar or Scipio?' How are you going to please them all? You reply:
• 'Caesar.' Go to **226**.
• 'Scipio.' Go to **197**.
• 'I don't care much one way or another.' Go to **221**.

211

Winesanspirix lets you down into the cellar through the trapdoor and closes it after you. From your hiding place, you hear the shop door open. 'Search everywhere, men!'

says the patrol leader. 'You two try the cellar. You three look in the charcoal store. The rest of you go upstairs.'
• Go to **216**.

212

This boar in wine is delicious. Yum, yum! There must be red wine and tomatoes in the sauce and cream and mushrooms and onions . . . you ought to get the recipe for Aunt Impedimenta. However, the legionaries aren't confining themselves to food; they've just been paid, and the wine flows freely. Empty amphoras litter the table. Suddenly one of them turns to you and offers you a glass. 'Have a drink, Gaul! Only XV years more to go in the army – we're celebrating!'
• You accept. Go to **195**.
• You refuse politely. Go to **210**.

213

You're doubtful. You can't imagine Vitalstatistix in this inn. It's not his style at all!
● You cross the road to visit the Invalid's Rest. Go to **202**.
● You set off for Gergovia. Go to **198**.

214

The Romans have arrested you all: Winesanspirix, his wife, Vitalstatistix and you. You didn't do very well, did you, Justforkix? You weren't worthy of the trust Getafix placed in you, and your rashness put your friends in danger. No, you aren't fit to be a Gaulish warrior, and YOUR ADVENTURE IS OVER – ingloriously.

215

The soldiers stand to attention as the officers arrive. 'Follow us to HQ, men! And you too, Gaul. You're involved in this too.'
● You obey. Go to **201**.
● You take a dose of magic potion and attack the three centurions. Go to **223**.

216

The trapdoor opens and two Roman soldiers come down into the cellar. They cast a rapid glance around them and go over to a barrel of wine. 'It's not worth searching this place,' says one of them. 'There's nobody here. Let's have a little drink!' 'Good idea,' says his companion. They sit down on the floor beside a barrel, take the bung out and drink several mugs of wine before going up again. 'Nobody down in the cellar, decurion!' they report. 'Nobody in the charcoal store either,' say the other legionaries. 'Right, let's go,' says the decurion. Winesanspirix tells you that the coast's clear; you can come up.
● Go to **225**.

217

A dozen Arvernians are sitting at a table greedily eating thick soup. They're making real pigs of themselves! You ask them for news of Vitalstatistix. 'Vitalstatistix? Never heard of him,' says one of them. 'You've got the wrong address. Too bad, son.'
● You go back to **229** and make another choice.

218

You sit down and enjoy an excellent boar in wine sauce. Aunt Impedimenta would be interested in the recipe. You amuse yourself by guessing what's gone into the sauce.
● Good – you feel refreshed and ready for the rest of your journey. Go to **229**.

219

You put a hand to your belt – and next thing you know you're seeing stars. That legionary certainly hits hard!
● You come round again at **199**.

220

The receptionist shows you into the atrium. Diagnostix the druid, who comes to meet you, is a tall, jovial man. Were you captured by the Romans and taken to the camp of Totorum at the beginning of your adventure?
● If you were, go to **196**.
●.If you weren't go to **209**.

221

'Don't get clever with us, Gaul! What do you really think?' asks the legionary, red with anger and alcohol. They're roaring drunk – and getting aggressive. Diplomacy is called for! You say:
- 'Caesar.' Go to **226**.
- 'Scipio.' Go to **197**.

222

YOU LOOK RATHER PALE TO ME, YOUNG MAN!

'Well, young man, what seems to be the trouble?' Diagnostix asks. You explain the rather complicated situation: Getafix has sent you to find your uncle Chief Vitalstatistix. It's a very important mission. 'Ah,' says the druid, 'so you're from my old friend Getafix's village too! It's a long time since I've had a chance to visit him. Vitalstatistix left us a week ago when he'd completed his treatment. He told me he was planning to visit some friends in Gergovia before he went home to his village. I strongly advised him against it! I mean, I can just see him going into all the best local inns. Arvernian cooking may have a great reputation, but your uncle's fragile liver isn't in any state to stand up to it.' Having gleaned this information:
- You set off for Gergovia straight away. Go to **198**.
- You begin your inquiries in one of the two inns in Aquae Calidae, the Invalid's Rest, at **202**.
- You decide to try the Thermal Springs Chariotel instead, at **213**.

223

Well done the magic potion! The other customers slip away, the innkeeper is protesting behind the bar, but your enemies have been knocked out without the slightest difficulty. You get out of the place fast, leaving behind you a scene of devastation . . . the least you can

I'M RUINED RUINED!

do is offer a sum as payment towards the damage (anything between 10 and 50 sestertii). *Subtract this sum of money from the contents of your purse.*
- Go to **229**.

224

Several Arvernians are sitting at a table talking as they eat sausage. You ask if any of them know Vitalstatistix. 'Vitalstatistix?' they say. 'No, don't know anyone of that name. You must have made a mistake.'
- You go back to **229** to make a different choice.

225

'You must leave Gergovia as fast as you can, before the Romans find you,' says Winesanspirix. 'Look, here are your things, and some provisions, and a slablet from the Gergovia Tourist Bureau with a map which should help you find your way out of town. Go out that way, and try not to get captured. Have a good journey – and I hope we meet again.'
- You go out into the street at **233**.

226

'You're right, Gaul! Julius Caesar's a good old Roman geezer!' roars the legionary, only to be interrupted by a well-aimed punch from his neighbour, a Scipio supporter. The third man takes advantage of the argument to tip the table over and threaten you with a chair. A person can't always stay neutral, especially when he has to fight for his life. In the confusion, you didn't notice the centurions come up.
- Go to **215**.

PAFF! BING!

227

- You go up to the bar to ask the innkeeper if Vitalstatistix has been here. Go to **231**.
- You order a boar in wine sauce. *The tables where you can sit to eat your meal have numbers on them. Each number corresponds to a paragraph.*

228

You take a deep breath, but guessing what you plan to do, the legionary presses his pilum harder against your stomach. 'Don't move, Gaul!' he warns.
- Resistance is useless. Go to **199**.

229

After several hours on the road . . . HOORAY! Gergovia at last! Geriatrix will be envious when he hears you've visited the scene of the Gaulish Resistance's finest hour. Do you remember the adventures Asterix had hereabouts?* Didn't he have a friend in Gergovia – a wine and charcoal merchant? Perhaps you've already learned his name in the course of your travels. Vitalstatistix is more than likely to have gone to see him – he may even still be there. You see four shops selling wines and charcoal along the street: where should you begin your inquiries? You can go:
- To see Winesanspirix, at **204**.
- To see Localpolitix, at **190**.
- To see Forinpolitix, at **224**.
- To see Thermostatix, at **217**.

*See ASTERIX AND THE CHIEFTAIN'S SHIELD.

230

THEY'RE IN A FILTHY MOOD!

Soon all the Romans are lying flattened on the charcoal. Phew! You're filthy - black from head to foot. But you can't wash the charcoal off now. Winesanspirix rushes in, out of breath. 'Quick!' he gasps. 'You must leave straight away, before the other Romans arrive. I'll tell them I didn't know you were hiding here. They'll think you got in through the cellar window when you saw a patrol in the street. Here's a map of Gergovia – it's a slablet produced by the tourist bureau. Get away as fast as you can! See you soon, I hope!'
- You go out into the street at **233**.

231

'A Gaulish warrior, not very fat, with red pigtails and an Armorican accent? Yes, of course, he dined here yesterday. No, I don't know where he was going. Sorry I can't help you any more.'
- Anxious to find your uncle as soon as possible, you leave the inn and go on your way. Go to **229**.
- A little boar in wine sauce wouldn't do any harm. Besides, it's a regional speciality, and they probably cook it better here than in the Arvernian restaurants of Lutetia. *You choose your table from the picture of the inn opposite and go to the corresponding paragraph.*

232

'Don't move, Gaul!' This is what's known as a rude awakening! Three Romans are pointing their pilums at your sternum, while a dozen others overpower Vitalstatistix. And standing behind the Roman soldiers you recognise the wine and charcoal merchant Thermostatix, with a nasty smile on his lips. The Romans are paying most attention to your uncle, Chief Vitalstatistix. You don't seem to impress them. (You can't think why not – a bold young Gaulish warrior like you!)
- You try to drink some magic potion. *Take a test of Skill (difficulty factor 4)*. If you fail, go to **219**. If you pass, go to **193**.
- You let them take you prisoner. Go to **214**.
- Stung to the quick, you fight the legionaries without taking any potion. Go to **228**.

CHAPTER V

IN FLIGHT

233

'I hope you've got a spot of magic potion left,' says Vital-statistix. 'I'm almost out of it myself – there's only a mouthful in my gourd! And Diagnostix advised me to lay off it anyway!' *(Remember that Vitalstatistix will be able to use his magic potion only once. Write that dose down on your Adventure Slab. You will be able to call on your uncle's physical qualities in fights, etc. His scores are 25 for Fighting Fitness and 10 for Skill.)* And now it's about time you left Gergovia. You keep close to the walls as you go along, because of the Roman soldiers patrolling the streets. You don't want to get involved in vulgar brawls with the enemy! Subtlety had better be your watchword, or you will run out of magic potion.

● *You and Vitalstatistix leave Winesanspirix's house; it is marked with a W on the map. Now you must leave the town.*

ROUTE

● *You choose your own route through the streets of Gergovia. Each number on the map corresponds to a paragraph.*

ON THE ALERT

● *Whenever you come to a road junction you throw the dice. If you throw 1, you have been spotted by a Roman patrol. To find out how many men are in the patrol, you throw two dice (or throw the dice twice if you have only one), add up the numbers you get, and then go to* **268.**

FIGHTS

● *The Fighting Fitness of a patrol depends on the number of Romans in it. Each of them has a Fighting Fitness score of 17; just multiply 17 by the number of legionaries. If the patrol consists of six or more men, the Romans automatically win the fight unless you take some magic potion.*

● *To fight a Roman patrol, set the total Fighting Fitness points of yourself and Vitalstatistix against the total Fighting Fitness points of the patrol, just as you would in ordinary single combat.*

● *Any Fighting Fitness points you or Vitalstatistix lose while still in Gergovia are not recovered until you have left the town.*

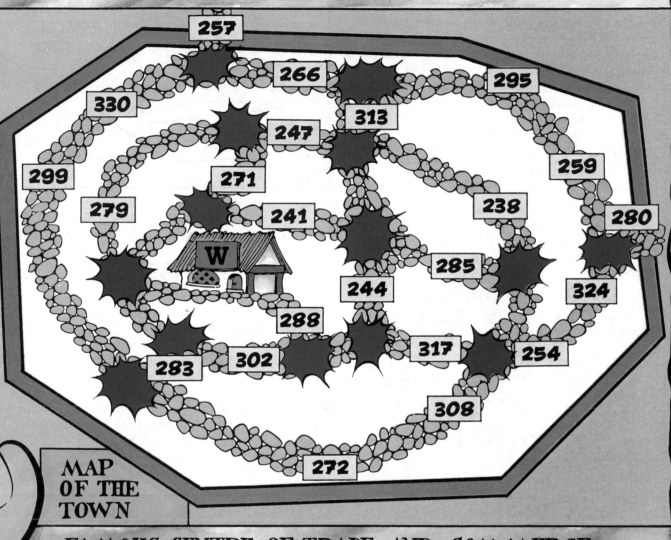

VISIT **GERGOVIA** IN THE ARVERNIAN COUNTRYSIDE

257
266
295
330
313
247
299
259
271
238
279
241
280
W
285
244
324
288
317
254
283
302
308
272

MAP OF THE TOWN

FAMOUS CENTRE OF TRADE AND COMMERCE

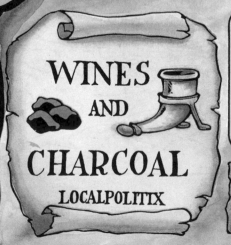

WINES AND CHARCOAL LOCALPOLITIX

FORINPOLITIX WINES AND CHARCOAL

WINES AND CHARCOAL THERMOSTATIX

WINESANSPIRIX WINES AND CHARCOAL

234

'Decurion!' shouts a legionary. 'Decurion, they're . . .' BOING! He has already gone flying over the fortifications, closely followed by his companions. The pair of you find yourselves alone, facing the stout wooden gates of the town. CREEAK! You put your shoulders to the gates and try forcing them, but they won't budge. They really are VERY stout. You'll have to take some more magic potion if you want to get out.

● Take a dose of potion, and the gates open at **298**.
● If you've run out of magic potion, or if you'd rather keep it in reserve, go back into Gergovia.

● Go to **248**.

237

You wake up lying in the corner between two houses, near the scene of the scuffle. The two mysterious Romans have disappeared without further explanation. Curious! You're wounded, and Vitalstatistix is a pitiful sight. However, you can't stay here. A patrol might easily spot you.

● After a few minutes' rest, and in spite of the sorry state you're both in, you decide to leave the town. *You and Vitalstatistix each get back 5 Fighting Fitness points.*

235

The Roman soldiers are marching down the road not far from you, led by a decurion. Being well disciplined, and pretty stupid too, they look straight ahead of them, noses in the air. They're not allowed to turn their heads – which is just as well for the two of you!

● A few minutes later, the patrol has disappeared down an alley, and you go on your way through Gergovia.

236

When you have knocked out the dozen or so legionaries guarding the gates of Gergovia, you see your Arvernian friend's head emerge from the bottom of the cart. Help – Vitalstatistix has disappeared! Oh no, he hasn't – he's still stuck in his barrel, and he's struggling to get free. Still under the effects of the potion, you pull it apart with your fingertips. Now you can both set off again. Once you're a little way out of town, your Arvernian friend stops. 'The coast's clear now,' he says. 'You can go on without me. Goodbye, and good luck!'

238

'Psst! Quick, this way! There are some Roman soldiers coming!' Someone is calling to you from a dimly lit passage between the houses.

● Followed by Vitalstatistix, go to **309**.
● Scenting a trap – experience counts for somthing, after all! – you take no notice and carry on. Go to **256**.

239

CRASH! You stumble and fall flat in the middle of the road. What with looking out for Romans to right and left of you, you forgot to watch where you were going! You hope to goodness the sound hasn't alerted them!
- You'll find out if it has at **268**.

240

The legionary points his pilum at you. Those wretched Arvernians . . . this is all because of their horrible accent! Why can't they talk normally, like people in Lutetia? There's no way of solving this by cunning now; you'll have to fight.
- You drink some magic potion. Go to **234**.
- If you have run out of potion, or you think you can do without it, go to **249**.

241

A Roman roadblock! The patrol is strung out right across the road – how will you ever get past them? *Throw the dice to find out how many legionaries there are.*
- With Vitalstatistix following in your wake, you attack the patrol. Go to **304**.
- You turn and go back on your tracks, hoping to find another way out of town. *Throw a dice. If you throw 1, go to* **268**. *If you throw 2 or more,* go on in another direction.

242

Trussed up like a couple of roast boars in a Lutetian delicatessen, you come round in a Roman tent, where two Gauls with hangdog expressions are talking to a Roman. 'Thanks to you,' says the Roman, 'we've captured the chief of those indomitable Gauls – oh, won't Caesar be pleased! We don't know who his young companion is, but we'll keep him prisoner too for the time being. Here's the 282 sestertii reward we promised – now, go!'
- Go to 316.

243

You take a good look at the fence; if you support yourself on the walls of the nearby houses, you should be able to get over it. You begin to climb. *Take a test of Skill for yourself (difficulty 3), and then another for Vitalstatistix.*
- If you both pass, go to **258**.
- If one of you fails, go to **329**.

244

What on earth made you decide to go this way? Here you are right outside the local Roman army headquarters! Hiding behind a house, you watch the Roman patrols march in and out. It's an impressive sight. Anyone can see Gergovia is an important centre of the Gaulish Resistance, and the Romans have stationed a large garrison here.

- You can't walk straight past. You turn round and retrace your steps before it's too late.
- Perhaps you'll find some way of leaving the town if you go inside. You attack the sentries and enter the building. Go to **314**.
- Looking casual, you stroll past the barracks . . . go to **322**.

245

Too bad! You'll have to fight. Vitalstatistix draws his sword and jumps down from the chariot. With your backs to a tree, you both fight fiercely. But there are a lot of Romans, and despite your courage and determination, your strength is beginning to ebb. To think of failing so near your goal!
- Go to **261**.

246

That was a close shave! The Romans of these parts are well nourished, as Obelix might say. Contrary to what you thought, the fight has not gone unobserved. Dozens of legionaries are already coming across the barracks square, making for you with pilums at the ready.

● You aren't going to retreat now, not after defeating so many big, solid legionaries. Nothing can withstand the magic potion. Go to **320**.

● Coming in here was a mistake. There's still time to escape to **318**.

247

You see the face of a pretty young girl at a window. Well, at least veterans of the siege aren't the only inhabitants of this town!

● Feeling more cheerful, you go on with your uncle.

248

'Right, let's go to Aquae Calidae,' says Vitalstatistix. 'We shall get home quickly in a chariot. I'm not too thrilled at the thought of meeting Chief Whosemorals-arelastix, but as it's protocol, I must. Sometimes responsibility weighs heavy on my shoulders, Justforkix . . . ah, well, tell me about your family, and Lutetia!' On reaching Aquae Calidae, Vitalstatistix goes to say good-bye to Diagnostix the druid, and gets lectured about his gastronomic follies.

AND HOW ABOUT YOUR LIVER, THEN?

● If you left your chariot at Aquae Calidae, go to **333**.
● If you sold it (or crashed it) you'll find one at **262**.

249

Gauls are the best-looking, strongest, bravest people in the world, and they fear only one thing, that the sky may fall on their heads tomorrow. Or so your uncle says. You're not quite so sure yourself. There are times when courage isn't a lot of help, particularly when you're facing a crowd of Roman soldiers armed to the teeth. Worn out, you both sink to the ground.

● The legionaries get hold of you at **316**.

250

'Are the Romans after you? Come into my house . . . there's a passage leading out of town. You can get out that way.'

● You trust the old man and follow him to **294**.
● You decline his offer and go on your way as before.

251

Soon the cart stops; it's reached a legion checkpoint*. 'Sorry, merchant, but we have orders to search all carts leaving Gergovia. What have you got in those barrels?' 'Wine, of course!' says the Arvernian. 'Wouldn't be carrying charcoal in them, would I?' 'Right. Repetitus, open up a barrel all the same and we'll make sure, or the decurion will have our guts for garters.' *There are six barrels on the cart. Choose two numbers between 1 and 6. The first is the barrel where you are hiding and the second is your uncle's barrel. Throw the dice to find out which barrel the legionary opens.*

● If the Roman opens the barrel where Vitalstatistix is hiding, go to **267**.

● If he inspects the barrel where you are hiding, go to **286**.

● If he searches one of the other barrels, go to **315**.

*Equivalent to a police checkpoint.

252

Once outside, you quickly put on your own clothes and take these uniforms off. They make you rather too conspicuous for your liking.

● And now it's time to set off for home, at **248**.

253

After going quite a way, the cart stops. Ouch! Something pricked your right side. Ouch! Something pricked your left side too. You can't move at all without being

injured. What's going on? Someone's clearing all the charcoal away, and to your surprise you find yourselves inside a Roman camp. The legionaries are keeping a respectful distance away, pilums trained on you. 'Resistance is useless – we've been betrayed!' says your uncle. 'You'd be speared before you could do a thing. We'll have to resign ourselves to captivity. Perhaps the village will be able to get by without me.' The centurion comes over. 'Well, Gauls!' he says. 'Not so full of ourselves now, eh? Oh, won't Caesar be pleased to know we've captured the chief of those indomitable Gauls! At long last I shall get to command a nice little century in a quiet suburb of Rome. As for you, merchant, here are 282 sestertii, and I don't want to hear any more of you!'
- Go to **316**.

254

An old Arvernian comes up and speaks to you. 'Is it you two the Romans are looking for everywhere? Come with me – I know a passage behind the ramparts. You can get out of Gergovia that way.'
- This sounds like a good way of escaping the Roman patrols. You follow him to **300**.
- It could be a trap. Better go on your way through Gergovia as before.

255

Getafix's magic potion again, eh? If you fought without drinking any, then you're certainly a doughty fighter! Well, the bandit can't do any more harm for the time being. During the scuffle, he dropped a small purse. You pick it up; it contains 10 sestertii, no doubt stolen from some other careless Gaul. Vitalstatistix comes round. 'What happened, 'Pedimenta dear?' he asks. 'Did the sky fall on my head? Oh, it's you, is it, lad? I'll be more careful in future. I shall go first, as befits a chief!'

- But for now Vitalstatistix has to walk beside you, leaning on your shoulder, because he is still rather dazed. *Until you get out of Gergovia, your uncle's Fighting Fitness points are reduced to 5.*

256

A cry makes you turn your heads. 'There they go, decurion!'
- Help! You're caught like rats in a trap. Go to **268**.

257

The town gates at last! But you're not out of trouble yet, there are twenty or so legionaries on guard. You haven't a hope of just walking through. If you can't make up your minds to use force, you'll have to go back into the town to think of some ruse that will get you past the patrol.
- You turn and go back into Gergovia.
- You both drink some magic potion *(strike out two doses on your Adventure Slab)*. Down with the enemy! Go to **234**.
- Boldly (or perhaps incautiously), you attack without taking any potion. Go to **249**.

258

Up on the ramparts, you glance down on the other side. No Romans in sight. And that nice little thicket down below will break your fall. You let yourselves drop from the top of the fortifications. Well done! You're out of Gergovia!
- Go to **248**.

259

Suddenly, at the corner of a road, you see more Roman soldiers. One of them, seeing you, says, 'Ssh! Keep quiet!' They seem to be rather nervous.
- Taking no notice of them, you go to **290**.
- You go up to one of the Romans and speak to him discreetly. Go to **326**.
- With your uncle in your wake, you attack. Go to **263**.

260

You look down from the top of the ramparts. OO-ER! You have to swallow hard. Keep calm! The fact is, you're on top of a cliff about thirty metres high. That's why the fence is lower in this part of town! You'll have to find some other way out.

• You go on your way through the town.

261

BOING! A menhir has just flattened the leader of the patrol. Obelix can't be far away – you know his methods. Sure enough, your friends come running out of the forest. 'Leave the Romans to us!' they beg. 'You must have had plenty all the way here!' The legionaries (not such fools as you might think) have taken advantage of this touching reunion to slip away. Obelix and Dogmatix pursue the Roman patrol all the same.

• Go to **328**.

262

Mecanix, the used chariot dealer near the town gates, sells you a large and quite fast wooden chariot for 40 sestertii. If you haven't got enough money left, Vitalstatistix will pay the difference.

• Go to **301**.

263

The legionaries have a Fighting Fitness score of 20 each, making a total of 40.
• If you win, go to **270**.
• If not, go to **237**.

264

Getting out of the barrel isn't easy, especially as the legionaries are seizing their chance to whack you over the head several times with the flat of their swords. When you finally manage to get to your feet, everything is going round and round! Resistance to all these legionaries would be useless. 'Well, Gauls, got you at last!'

says the patrol leader, with great satisfaction. 'Caesar will be ever so pleased, and I'll get promoted to centurion.' You are bound and taken to the nearby Roman camp of Humdrum.

• Got to **316**.

265

You cautiously go a little further, backs to the wall. Once you have made sure there is no patrol nearby, you go on your way through Gergovia.

266

Take a test of Skill (difficulty 3) for Vitalstatistix.
• If he fails, go to **331**.
• If he passes, *you take one too*. If you succeed as well, go to **310**. If you fail, go to **239**.

267

Crouched in your barrel, heart thudding, you hear a Roman say, 'Come here, Papyrus, Citrus, Eucalyptus, everyone! I've got one! Don't you move, merchant, or it'll be the worse for you!' They must have found Vitalstatistix. In no time they are taking the top off your barrel as well and you hear the Roman say, 'And here's another!'

• You surrender without a fight. Go to **264**.
• You drink some magic potion and emerge from your barrel, smashing it with one thrust of your shoulder. Go to **236**.
• You don't take any magic potion, but try to get up and fight the legionaries, counting on your Uncle Vitalstatistix's aid. Go to **289**.

268

'Get them, men!' The Romans have seen you, but there is enough distance between you and them to give you a choice of action.

• You turn and face them, ready to fight. Go to **304**.
• You decide to cut and run, hoping to shake them off. Go to **318**.

269

A dozen legionaries are on guard at the gates of Gergovia. 'Hey there, Gauls! Who are you, and where are you off to in such a hurry?' You pretend to be Arvernians, and imitate an Arvernian accent. 'We're from the second shop down the street over there, and we're going out to pick mushrooms.' *Have they been taken in by your attempts to imitate the local accent?*
• Go to **293** to find out.

WE'RE ARVERNIANS
FROM THE STREET
OVER THERE,
GOING OUT TO
PICK MUSHROOMS

270

The sight of the two legionaries flat out on the ground by the walls of the houses gives you a brilliant idea. Why not put their uniforms on and leave Gergovia disguised as Roman soldiers?
• You really do get some good ideas now and then! What does your uncle think of this one? Go to **281**.
• No, it's too risky. You give up the notion and go on your way.

271

A rather drunk Roman soldier is lying in the street with an empty amphora beside him.

• There's a risk he may notice you and raise the alarm. You catch hold of your uncle's sleeve, turn, and go on your way.
• Considering the state he's in, there's no danger. You walk on as if he weren't there at all. *Throw a dice.* If you get 1, 2 or 3, go to **311**. If you throw 4, 5 or 6, go to **276**.

272

The road runs beside the wooden fence built by the Romans. The ramparts don't look quite so high here.
• This is a chance not to be missed. You and Vitalstatistix try to climb the ramparts and get down the other side, outside the town. Go to **312**.
• You might be spotted climbing the fence. Better go on your way through the town.

273

The patrol passes you at a fast trot, but at the last moment someone calls, 'Decurion, they're hiding there!' You can't run for it this time. You'll have to fight.
• Go to **304**.

274

You go past the houses in the darkness, stepping across piles of rubbish and trying not to tread on the chickens that keep getting in your way.

• You finally come out in the road going along beside the ramparts and continue on your way. *Throw a dice to find out where you get. If you throw 1 or 2, you end up between numbers 283 and 272; if you throw 3 or 4, you end up between numbers 272 and 308; if you throw 5 or 6, you end up between numbers 308 and 254. Carry on from the place where you come out.*

275

The Romans are soon lying about all over the place. Some of them have even landed on the rooftops of neighbouring houses. You are amused to see Arvernians putting their heads out of their windows, and looking very impressed. But there's no time to be lost; you must leave the town.
• Having got rid of that obstacle, you go on your way.

276

'Hey, lads – hic! – the Gauls are – hic! – here!' yelps the legionary, getting to his feet with difficulty. Soon there are several Romans on the spot. *Throw two dice to find out how many.*

- Go to **268**.

277

'Are the Romans looking for you? Yes, of course you can come up in my cart! Hide in the two empty barrels at the back.' That's all right for you, but easier said than done for Vitalstatistix, considering his weight. The driver of the cart is getting impatient. 'Hurry up, for goodness' sake, or we'll be spotted!' he says. Your uncle finally manages to get into his barrel, and the cart sets off again towards the town gates.

- Go to **251**.

278

The cart stops, and an animated discussion between the Roman soldiers takes place . . .

> WE'D BETTER SEARCH THE CONTENTS OF THIS CART.

> ARE YOU CRAZY, BY MERCURY? WE'LL GET FILTHY, AND THERE'S A KIT INSPECTION COMING UP – POLISHED CALIGAE AND ALL THAT!

- Phew! The cart sets off again, at **315**.

279

Keeping close to the walls of the Arvernian houses, you make your way forward. Vitalstatistix follows you in silence. A door opens behind you, and a whisper close to your ear makes you jump. 'Quick, come and hide in

here! There's a Roman patrol coming! You can leave again when they've gone by!'

- Suspicious, you ignore the invitation. Go to **265**.
- You enter the house. Go to **291**.

280

'By Belisama!' Vitalstatistix whispers. 'The gates are closed!' He is right. The Romans have closed the heavy wooden gates of the fortified town. Anyone who wants to go out has to pass a dozen legionaries on sentry duty. There's no hope of slipping by them incognito.

- You turn and go on your way through the streets of Gergovia.
- You both drink some magic potion (*strike out two doses from those remaining*) and then make for the gate. Go to **234**.
- You attack without magic potion – it'll be like the great victory of Gergovia all over again! Go to **249**.

281

'What, me, a Gaulish chieftain – dress up as a Roman soldier? Never!' cries Vitalstatistix. 'Oh, well . . . maybe I will after all, if it's for the good of the village . . .' You take off your Gaulish clothes and put on the Roman uniforms. Your uncle has some trouble getting into his breastplate and hiding his pigtails under the regulation Roman helmet. 'Uncle Vitalstatistix,' you point out, 'Roman soldiers don't wear whiskers! You'll have to cut your moustache off, or they'll spot us at once!' 'Look here, lad,' says your uncle, 'there are depths to which I will not sink. Whoever saw a Gaul without a moustache? It's my duty as a chief to respect Gaulish traditions!' *Take a test of Charm (difficulty 3) to see if you can persuade Vitalstatistix to cut his moustache off.*

- If you succeed, go to **323**.
- If you fail, go to **307**.

282

'Vitalstatistix, I doubt if your whiskers will have grown again before the meeting,' says the druid thoughtfully. 'And a Gaulish chieftain can hardly take part in official

ceremonies without a fine moustache. Chief Whose-moralsarelastix might be shocked if you didn't respect protocol! I'll see if I can find the recipe for a potion I used a few years ago when Asterix and I were prisoners of the Romans in the fortified camp of Totorum*. And Justforkix – you did very well to complete a mission which turned out rather more difficult than I foresaw.'

● Go to **334.**

*See ASTERIX THE GAUL.

283

A roadblock! There are Romans in position right across the street. *Throw two dice to find out exactly how many there are.*

● Sweeping Vitalstatistix along with you, you decide to attack the patrol. Go to **304.**

● It seems more sensible to turn back. But you may already have been spotted. *Throw a dice. If you throw 1* go to **268.** *If you throw 2 or more*, carry on in a different direction.

284

Vitalstatistix jumps down from the cart. You soon catch up with the Romans. But you have hardly knocked one of them out when all of a sudden . . .

● Go to **261.**

285

Followed by your uncle, you go down the narrow alley. You are keeping under cover in the shadow of the Arvernian houses, so there's not much risk of the Romans taking you by surprise. BONK! You hear the sound of something falling behind you. You turn round. What a sight! Vitalstatistix is lying on the ground, unconscious. And you yourself are facing a mountain of a man armed with an enormous club: a brigand! You're trembling like a leaf! *With your uncle out for the count, you*

will have to tackle this formidable opponent on your own. His Fighting Fitness score is 30.

● If you win the fight, go to **255.**

● If you lose, go to **321.**

286

The lid is lifted off your barrel. 'Don't move, Gaul!' says the Roman soldier, drawing his sword.

● From a position of such weakness, you can only surrender without a fight. Go to **264.**

● You take a dose of your magic potion and emerge from your barrel at **236.**

● You get up and attack the legionaries without any magic potion. Go to **289.**

287

'Hi there,' says the Arvernian. 'I'm Rheumatix and this is my brother Aromatix. We know the Romans are after you, and we'd be happy to help you get out of Gergovia. The Romans know us well – they see us go out of town every day to pick mushrooms. If you put on some of our clothes as a disguise, and blackened your whiskers with some charcoal, they'd never notice a thing!'

● Good idea! These Arvernians aren't such fools as they look. You dress up as Arvernians and make for the town gates. Go to **269.**

● You're not going to fool about with disguises. You go on your way.

288

A black cat crosses the road in front of you. Vitalstatistix taps you on the shoulder. 'That's bad luck, Justforkix. We'd better go back.'

● You can either go on or turn back.

289

Alone against more than ten legionaries, you tire, stagger, and fall to the ground. The barrel containing Vital-statistix is swaying to and fro – why doesn't he come out? When the Roman soldiers have tied you up they turn to your uncle, who is jammed inside his barrel. What bad luck! (Especially if he had any magic potion left.)
• You and Vitalstatistix find yourselves at **316**.

290

The Romans must know their friends are looking for you all over the city. And yet they let you by as if they had no idea of it . . . no doubt about it, these Romans are crazy!
• You go on your way through Gergovia.

291

BONK! You feel a nasty blow on your head.
• You are knocked unconscious, and wake up at **242**.

292

What to all appearances is a spot of civil war turns out to be an unequal struggle, since Roman soldiers can't do a thing against Gauls stuffed with magic potion. Once you've sent them flying over the fence, so that they crash to the ground on the other side, you put your shoulders to the gates, force them open, and leave Gergovia.
• Go to **252**.

293

Has your story about being Arvernians going to pick mushrooms been accepted? You wait in suspense . . .
• The Romans are rather suspicious of your Arvernian accent. Go to **240**.
• Your accent was perfect. Go to **327**.

294

The old man lets you into a shop which reminds you of Winesanspirix's place. 'I'm Localpolitix,' he says, 'and I sell wines and charcoal. It's a pleasure to lend a hand to fellow Gauls fleeing from the Romans. Follow me – the passage starts in my cellar.' You go down to his cellar in single file. A barrel of wine is pushed aside, revealing the entrance to a tunnel. After groping your way along it for a few minutes, you emerge in the open, behind a bush. Not a Roman in sight! You are out of Gergovia. Well done!
• Go to **248**

295

The road goes on, keeping close to the town walls. You make your way cautiously forward, backs to the fence. Suddenly Vitalstatistix taps you on the shoulder, and whispers, 'Laddie, I think we could get over the ramparts if we climbed them there, over by that house.'
• You try climbing. Go to **243**.
• You decide you'd rather carry on to the town gates, which can't be much farther now, and you go on your way through Gergovia.

296

'We're legionaries Justforcicus and Vitalstatisticus, on our way to Aquae Calidae with a message for Centurion Somniferus,' you say. And you pass the roadblock set up at the city gates without the slightest trouble. It was a truly BRILLIANT idea!
• Go to **252**.

297

Having done your duty, you go back up into the shop. The Arvernian who lured you into this trap has gone.
• You leave the house and cautiously continue on your way.

298

Ahead of you lie the Arvernian moutains and the road to Aquae Calidae, and there isn't a Roman in sight. You're out of Gergovia! Congratulations; it wasn't all that easy!
• Go to **248**.

299

You try to get by unnoticed. A window opens on the other side of the street, and a man beckons.
• He probably wants to help you. You cross the road to hear what he has to say. Go to **250**.
• Better not take any risks. You carry on along the street of the town.

300

'It's an old secret tunnel built during the Gallic War. It runs underground from the cellar of my house and comes out on the other side of the ramparts. The Romans have forgotten its existence,' says the man. He guides you into a shop with a sign saying 'Wines and Charcoal', and opens the trapdoor to the cellar. You both go down, and suddenly you hear a click behind you. The trapdoor has closed again. What's going on?

COME THIS WAY!

• The Arvernian must have heard a Roman patrol coming and closed the trapdoor. You must find the way into the underground tunnel before the legionaries think of searching this cellar. You start looking behind the barrels of wine. Go to **332**.
• This is probably a trap. Better open the trapdoor again and get out of here, before the traitor brings half the garrison down on you. Go to **325**.

301

A little later you pass through Condatum, and after three days' uneventful journey, you arrive in Armorica. How glad you are to be returning to the little Gaulish village! Vitalstatistix is thinking of the banquet at the end of your adventure. But never rest on your laurels – all of a sudden a Roman patrol appears round a bend in the path in the forest surrounding the village . . .
• One of you takes another does of magic potion – maybe the last? Go to **284**.
• You don't have any potion left. Go to **245**.

302

Your uncle tugs your sleeve. 'Why don't we try going this way, lad?' Sure enough, there is a small, squalid-looking alley leading to the south of the town. You didn't spot it before.
• The Romans aren't likely to be patrolling narrow alleys like this, so here's a good way of escaping them. If you decide to go along the alley, go to **274**.
• You could get lost in this labyrinth of narrow alleys, not to speak of the danger of falling into a trap. Better continue on your way along the streets of Gergovia.

303

'All's well that ends well,' says Getafix the druid. He sounds pleased. 'Chief Whosemoralsarelastix will have to admit that our own chief always honours his obligations. And congratulations, Justforkix! You've successfully completed a mission which turned out more difficult than I expected.'
• Go to **334**.

304

Two Gauls against a Roman patrol: fair odds! *Throw the dice to find out how many legionaries you are facing.*

● Two of you – well, that counts as being numerically superior, not that it prevents one of you taking a dose of magic potion to make sure he's on top form. Go to **275**.

● You've run out of potion, or you'd rather save it. If you win the fight without any magic potion, go to **319**. If you're defeated, go to **249**.

305

BOING! One thrust of your shoulder sends the trapdoor flying across the room, along with the chest that was keeping it closed. You go up the steps and find yourself in the shop. It is empty, but glancing out of the window, you see your supposed friend the Arvernian merchant talking to the leader of a Roman patrol. There's no doubt about it – you've been betrayed. 'In Gergovia, at that,' sighs Vitalstatistix.

● You get out into the street though the opposite window, steal quietly away, and then go on as before.

306

'Hurry up, do, or they'll spot us!' says your helpful friend. You jump into the cart, followed by Vitalstatistix. Both of you burrow into the load of charcoal just as a Roman patrol appears round the corner of the road. Phew! They haven't seen you. The cart goes on along the road, swaying from side to side, although down there in the dark you're not too sure just where you are. *Throw a dice.*

● If you throw 1, 2 or 3, go to **278**.

● If you throw 4 or more, go to **253**.

307

Disguised as Romans, you set off towards the town gates, where you identify yourselves. 'Legionaries Justforcicus and Vitalstatisticus, on our way to Aquae

Calidae with a message for Centurion Somniferus.' The Roman soldiers on sentry duty at the town gates take your word for it and start waving you on. But all of a sudden one of them turns, points to Vitalstatistix's moustache and says, 'Hey – you're not legionaries at all! You're Gauls! They're Gauls! Get them!' And you find yourselves facing fifteen Romans.

● If either of you uses the magic potion, go to **292**.

● If not, go to **249**.

308

A cart full of barrels of wine and drawn by two horses passes in front of you.

● This is a chance not to be missed! You ask the driver of the cart if you can hide under the barrels and get out of the town that way. Go to **277**.

● The Romans are sure to search all vehicles leaving the town, not to mention that you'd also risk having the driver denounce you. No, you'd better find some other way out. You carry on along the streets of Gergovia.

309

'Come this way – follow me!' an old Arvernian tells you. 'The Romans are everywhere these days! We'll have to throw them out like we did in '52, at the time of the siege. Ah, those were the days, those were!' He guides you through the narrow alleys, and you find yourselves in a parallel road, *between numbers 295 and 259 (use these numbers only to visualise the place on the map where you come out).*

● You go on through Gergovia.

310

Phew! You nearly tripped over a stone in the middle of the road. Why don't you look where you're going? Watch where you put your feet!

● You carry on along the city streets.

311

HIC! HAEC! HOC!

'Cheers – hic! – all, and so – haec! – says all of us – hoc!' says the legionary, as you pass by.
● You go on along the streets of Gergovia.

312

You inspect the ramparts. It will be difficult to climb them, but there's no such word as 'impossible' in the Gaulish language. So you start climbing, with Vitalstatistix close on your heels. *Take a test of Skill (difficulty 3) for yourself, and then another test for your uncle.*
● If you both succeed, go to **260.**
● If one of you fails, go to **329.**

313

Very clever! The Romans have set up a roadblock across the main street of Gergovia. Throw two dice to find out exactly how many men you are facing.
● Taking Vitalstatistix with you, you decide to attack the patrol. Go to **304.**
● It seems more sensible to turn back. *Throw a dice. If you throw 1, go to **268.** If you throw 2 or more,* carry on along your way, but in another direction.

314

The two Roman soldiers on sentry duty outside the barracks obviously belong to an elite troop. They are gigantic! The sight of them makes you shake in your shoes.

Even having the magic potion doesn't reassure you. *The Romans have a Fighting Fitness score of 30 each. The outcome of the fight is worked out by comparing the total of your own Fighting Fitness points with the Fighting Fitness of the two legionaries, i.e. 60. Throw the dice.*
● If you win, with or without the potion, go to **246.**
● If not, go to **316.**

315

The cart is going faster now, and as you can't hear the sound of cobblestones under its wheels any more, you guess you have left Gergovia. A few minutes later, the merchant stops and you emerge from your hiding place.

'There's the road to Aquae Calidae,' he says. 'No, don't thank me, it's only right and natural to help one's fellow countrymen. Goodbye and good luck!'
● Go to **248.**

316

You haven't done too well, Justforkix! You weren't worthy of Getafix's trust in you, and it's your fault Vitalstatistix has been captured. Asterix and Obelix, however, are real heroes, and they'll soon rescue the pair of you. But YOUR ADVENTURE IS OVER!

317

A Roman patrol strung out right across the road is checking all passers-by. Unless you are going to use force, you will have to turn back. *Throw two dice to find out how many men there are in the patrol.*
● Taking Vitalstatistix with you, you decide to attack the patrol. Go to **304.**
● It seems more sensible to turn back. *Throw a dice. If you throw 1, go to **268.** If you throw 2 or more,* carry on along your way, but in another direction.

318

PFFFF! PFFFF!

The Romans may not be as fast as you are, but Vitalstatistix is easily the heaviest and slowest, especially without the shieldbearers who usually carry him round. The beneficial effects of his treatment at Aquae Calidae are already wearing off. You can't outstrip the Romans. On the other hand, you can hide in the doorway of an Arvernian house, praying to the gods that no one will notice you. *Throw a dice.*

- *If you throw 1, 2 or 3, go to* **273.**
- *If you throw 4, 5 or 6, go to* **235.**

319

Phew! You're out at last. The Romans have collapsed all over the road behind you. You're both worn out; better avoid meeting any more legionaries just now. 'Laddie, Gaul can be proud of us!' says Vitalstatistix as you take him by the sleeve and start off again. *NB – you neither of you get your Fighting Fitness points back until you have left Gergovia.*

320

BIFF! PAF! PAAF!! BOING! CRAAAASH!

Even full of magic potion, two Gauls can't do much against several hundred Roman soldiers. Your uncle is strong, of course, but not as strong as Obelix. And just as you are about to take a dose of magic potion, you see that there is a hole in the gourd.

- After putting up a brave fight, you are defeated by superior numbers. Go to **316.**

321

Still feeling dazed, you slowly become aware of reality again. You are tied up and hanging head downwards over the giant's shoulder – and Vitalstatistix is slung over his other shoulder. You soon come to a Roman camp. The brigand throws you to the ground like a couple of ordinary parcels outside the centurion's tent. 'Me capture two outlaws!' he announces in bad Latin. 'Me get reward – get loadsa sestertii!'

- Go to **316.**

322

Keeping your heads down, and skirting the walls, you go past the barracks keeping in the shadow of the houses. *Take a test of Skill (difficulty 3) for yourself, and then another for Vitalstatistix.*

- If at least one of you fails, the sentries spot you as you pass within a few paces of them, and you have to fight them at **314.**
- If you both pass, you get by without being noticed and go on your way through the streets of Gergovia.

323

'Oh, all right, if I must! A Gaulish chieftain must sacrifice what he holds most dear for the good of his village. You are the witness of my heroism!' And sadly, Vitalstatistix takes out his knife and CUTS OFF HIS MOUSTACHE! As you walk on, he keeps complaining. 'These caligae hurt horribly, this pilum weighs a ton, this breastplate's much too tight, this tunic makes me look fat . . .'

- Go to **296.**

324

'Psst! This way, quick!' You see a skinny Arvernian calling to you through an open door.
- You have almost reached the town gates now. There's no point in taking risks. You go on your way.
- He probably wants to help you. You go into the house. Go to **287**.

WELL, COMING?

325

'Ouff! By Belenos, this wretched trapdoor won't budge!' says your uncle. He is right; you push too, as hard as you can, but without success. *Take a test of Fighting Fitness (difficulty 4) for yourself and one for Vitalstatistix.*
- If one of you passes, go to **305**.
- If in spite of all your efforts you can't move the trapdoor, go to **332**.
- Or if you fail you could decide to take a dose of magic potion. In that case go to **305**.

326

'We've deserted from the garrison of Gergovia and we want to go home to Latium. We know there are legionaries after you – but listen, we can help you! We're prepared to swap our uniforms for your Gaulish clothes. Then we can all leave the town incognito.'
- You accept this offer. Go to **281**.
- You would rather keep your Gaulish identity, and go on your way.

327

'Pass, friend!' says the legionary, putting on a strong Arvernian accent himself. Is he by any chance laughing at you? As soon as you're out of sight of the Roman soldiers, you take off your Arvernian clothes.
- Go to **248**.

328

Back in the village, Getafix welcomes you with open arms! 'Justforkix! Vitalstatistix! Here you are at last! And not before time! Chief Whosemoralsarelastix, on learning that our chief was away, was preparing to break the traditional bonds between our two villages and get in touch with the Romans, using your absence from the meeting as an excuse. We were really worried.' Has Vitalstatistix cut his moustache off?
- If he has, go to **282**.
- If his moustache is intact, go to **303**.

329

By Belenos, what a fall! You tumble to the ground, dragging each other along. Vitalstatistix seems to have injured his leg, and is in no state to try the climb again. Suddenly a Roman patrol appears round the corner of the street, attracted by the dull thud of your fall. With his injured leg, Vitalstatistix can't run for it. You must fight. *Throw two dice to find out how many Roman soldiers you are facing. Vitalstatistix's injury takes 3 points off your Fighting Fitness score. You can take a dose of magic*

potion if you have any left.
- If you win the fight, you go on your way through Gergovia.
- If you are beaten, go to **249**.

330

A cart full of charcoal, driven by an old Arvernian, goes swaying down the street, making for the town gates. There's no patrol in sight – you'd better take advantage of that fact . . .
- Here's a chance not to be missed. You ask the driver of the cart if you can hide in the charcoal and get out of town that way. Go to **306**.
- You don't think this Arvernian looks very honest. Better go on your way and think of some other cunning way of getting out.

331

BOING! You hear something thud to the ground beside you. In spite of his new slim figure (well, relatively slim), your uncle has just tripped over a stone and fallen full length in the street. If you go on like this you'll be picked up before you know it!
- Go to **268**.

332

'Well, Gauls, you're caught like rats in a trap!' The trap-door above has opened, and it is a Roman decurion who dares to address you in such terms. 'I'll teach him

manners, I will!' roars Vitalstatistix, advancing to the fray. 'I'll show him the difference between a Gaul and a rat!' There is no other way out of the cellar, so you have to fight. *Throw two dice to find out how many legionaries you are facing.*
- If you win, go to **297**.
- If you don't then sad to say, you must go to **249**.

333

You pick your chariot up again in Aquae Calidae. The horses look as if they've been taking the same course of treatment as Vitalstatistix; they're very thin. You'll buy them a nice feed of oats at the next service station – they deserve it. And now you set off for the little village!
- Go to **301**.

334

That evening a great banquet is held in honour of the chief's return (and yours!). Under the starry sky, everyone is in cheerful mood. You all drink plenty of wine and cider, and eat dozens of roast boar. This time it's you, Justforkix, who has stories of Gergovia to tell Geriatrix. Asterix is glad to hear news of his friend Winesanspirix. Getafix asks about the latest methods of treatment at Aquae Calidae and the health of his colleague Diagnostix. Between boars, Obelix expresses anxiety about the quality of Arvernian air (he has heard it's good for wild boar and Romans). You try hard to disentangle the various boar recipes you told yourself you'd bring back for Aunt Impedimenta's benefit. The whole village is proud of you – a young Lutetian who has behaved like a true Gaulish warrior. The singing and dancing goes on all night long . . . and by the way, what's happened to the bard?

PRINTED IN BELGIUM BY
proost
INTERNATIONAL BOOK PRODUCTION